THE SHOOTING SCRIPT®

THIS IS 40

Also by Judd Apatow

Newmarket Shooting Scripts
Funny People: The Shooting Script
Knocked Up: The Shooting Script

THIS IS 40

SCREENPLAY BY
JUDD APATOW

INTRODUCTION BY LENA DUNHAM

newmarket press
for itbooks
AN IMPRINT OF HARPERCOLLINS PUBLISHERS

A Newmarket Shooting Script® Series Book

FIRST EDITION

Library of Congress Cataloging-in-Publication Data is available upon request.

ISBN 978-0-06-226739-9

12 13 14 15 16 10 9 8 7 6 5 4 3 2 1

CONTENTS

BY LENA DUNHAM

There are many reasons why we write. Some of us write for glory—to spite the people who stuffed us in lockers, to remind the lovers who did-n't love us just what they're missing out on, to alter history and have future generations sing our names.

Others write for money (probably a weird plan, even when it does work out).

But some of us, as Judd reminded me in a recent e-mail, "write to fig-ure something out."

I've been working with Judd for two and a half years now. From the first time we met, in the intimidating lobby of a midtown hotel where he set me at ease by wearing his socks pulled up very high, I was dazzled and comforted by the speed with which he turns his experiences into art. I have always felt vaguely sociopathic because I will often be living something (such as, I don't know, stressful sex) and writing the outline of it in my head at the very same moment. Then I force my family and friends to act out my former humiliations. Well, if that's sociopathic, then Judd and I are the same kind of sociopath; but through watching him work, I began to suspect that it was not a social disease but rather an attempt to get our hands around the wriggly, terrifying monster that is human interaction.

As a young filmmaker, I was given the gift of witnessing every step of Judd's process with *This Is 40*. I was allowed in, and I felt like a bull in a china shop, unable to believe he would truly want the feedback of a first-timer with a poor grasp of Final Draft software. From our first meeting in his office, when he showed me notes for the script written in his smart-phone and on assorted crumpled papers like an old-timey scientist's, to the test screening, where I was so nervous I ate three hot dogs and kicked J. J.

Abrams, I felt the film come together, and I stole the lessons of its creation to use for my own wayward purposes. And although much has been made of Apatow's mania for improv, what he actually does is rewrite the script as we go.

As I struggled to crack the *Girls* pilot, Judd diverted me with the first scenes of his soon-to-be movie. One of the earliest was the Viagra birthday-sex scene ("I thought you'd think it was fun for me to supersize it for once"). I laughed and laughed. Little did I know, Judd would soon have me directing a way parents-ier sex scene. (On a sidenote, Judd reading his own script aloud is, as Martha Stewart would say, a very good thing. His Albert Brooks voice is better than Albert Brooks's own.) My first impression of the script for *This Is 40* was that it was doing what I believe is the primary job of art: clarifying something we all know is there, but that has not yet been illuminated and normalized for us. And when you work from life, the material is boundless.

Judd woke up every day at home with Maude, Iris, and Leslie, and the script grew and grew with the specific foibles of a man sharing a life with three dynamic, wicked women. But the movie is not Judd's life—as he always says, a third is real, a third observations, and a third fabrications (which makes me want to up my game, as I use only about an eighth fabrications). I watched Judd do the hard work of story, sculpting a narrative from the fabric of the day-to-day, killing his darlings, who, in this case, are his actual darlings. I watched him cheerfully receive countless sets of notes from more people than I could ever stomach notes from. But he can handle it because, intuitively, he knows what to take, and he leaves the rest on the pyre. It requires confidence not to be swayed from your path by dissonant voices. As a result I stopped shutting the peanut gallery out of my own work, and I was all the better for it.

I watched Judd cast the film. (He even cast me, though only one and a half of my five scenes remain.) At the center, Paul and Leslie have a strange magic. Strange because he is not her real-life husband, not the real-life father of her real-life on-screen children (can you follow that?), but when the cameras were rolling she looked at him with all the passion and disdain you would direct at the love of your life. They perfectly replicate the dynamic of battered soul mates, to the point that I have to look away occasionally, even on viewing number eleven.

I visited the set and sat behind Judd as he mouthed the words right along with his actors and then huddled with Leslie, pitching and clarifying. I saw Leslie and Judd, as a team, create material, question it, and then improve it. She put him through his paces in a way that was both wifely and creatively rigorous. Together they would take a moment from real life and make it something utterly new—and this is just the kind of murky act that intrigues me most. A moment that stands out for me is the monologue in which Debbie announces, "I've wasted my whole life busting the balls of people who have no balls!" She showcases Judd's determination to balance the film, to give the women in the audience something to cheer about. The fact that he wants that makes me want to stand up and cheer—so much so that I broke up with a boyfriend because I couldn't imagine us sharing a creative exchange like the ones I was witnessing. (Also, Leslie caught me semi-sexting on set. I have to say it here and shed the shame.)

I have as much to say about this movie as Judd does about his life because of the way he let me in.

My first version of this intro was a quippy, concept-heavy farce about Judd attempting to write a screenplay but instead just eating boatloads of ice cream while the world turned into a crazy Hieronymus Bosch painting all around him. It was heavy on jokes and light on content, and it broke what I've learned is the cardinal rule of Apatow writing: let's get at something. It doesn't matter how clever the structure. As Judd said to me in another recent e-mail on another topic altogether: "We want to try to be more than just amusing here."

ON THE SET

BY GRAHAM PARKER

"Be outside the hotel at 5:50 A.M.," said the e-mail that night. What? Are we going fishing? And there were more of them like that, too. Getting to know dawn in Los Angeles is something I've only experienced before from the wrong side of it, if you know what I mean. Well, I had to hand it to these Hollywood types: they were certainly working for a living.

Walking onto the set that first day—the "Backyard Bar-B-Que" scene—where Pete (Paul Rudd) celebrates his birthday, was intimidating to say the least. Just about the first thing I saw was John Lithgow picking through some food items on a table with a bunch of other fine actors following him, as he uttered words from the script verbatim, absolutely flawlessly, moving along and forking up items onto his plate like it was some kind of ballet. No, this is not right. I shouldn't be here, I was thinking. I'll just quietly back out of the place, slip out to the street before anyone sees me, get a cab back to the hotel, get my stuff, go to the airport, and get the fuck out of here before I make a complete twit of myself. Yes, that's the sensible thing to do.

I've been hired . . . as an actor? What?

But it's too late, the jig is up. Someone resembling Albert Brooks has just appeared in front of me, and apparently I'm talking to him, pretending to understand what the heck he's saying, pretending that this is all very normal.

Time becomes elastic, bendy, like a Dali painting, and then Judd Apatow, or a fellow pretending to be him, is giving me incomprehensible instructions: something about walking across the lawn, smiling at a tiny lady, who may be Nicaraguan, who will offer me a sweetmeat on a tray, which I will take, smiling back, and as this complicated event is taking place, Pete, aka Paul Rudd, will suddenly appear and come crashing between us, and I'm supposed to then follow his exit with my eyes in a vaguely questioning manner, because he's probably not very happy with me because I'm bringing his record company to the brink of ruin, because my music is extraordinarily unpopular. And then I have to continue walking across the lawn as if this were something any ordinary person could do, like no biggie, right?

At least that's what I think I was told to do. I didn't think anyone could do so many things in such short space of time. What am I, a contortionist or something? Oh, it may sound easy to you, but at the time it felt like I'd just been told to give a dissertation to Albert Einstein on how he'd bollixed up the theory of relatively and had actually written a recipe for fruitcake. (Being told to walk past Megan Fox and look down her dress, as I was later, was much easier. That I could do.) And apparently cameras are recording this, although I refuse to look at them, because knowing where they are and what they're doing will make me blow this like almost every other pop singer who tries to act and ends up mugging, like they're doing a bloody MTV video or something.

But, hey, the lunches were free and quite awesome, so I became determined to become an actor, in order to drag this thing out for as long as possible, in order to have more free lunches, and by my second attempt I was starting to get the hang of it. Not because I'm any good, but because I was channeling my father, who was a very funny bloke. (I'd like to say he was looking down on me, chuckling, but he couldn't have been, because he's dead.)

Well, that's acting, isn't it? Pretend to be someone else! Yep, I think I've got it. . . .

Q & A

FIVE OBVIOUS QUESTIONS
FOR JUDD APATOW

Why did you write this?

I do believe in the old saying "we write the movie to figure out why we are writing the movie." I started out as someone who just wanted to write comedy. I never thought about comedy being an intimate, vulnerable act. Lately I have accepted that writing is a form of self-exploration. I am trying to sort through how I feel about this life while attempting to make it amusing on some level. When I wrote *Funny People* my mom had just died from ovarian cancer, and the purpose of life was something I was struggling with, so I had the need to write about it. I am not sure if it was a form of healing or denial, but I seemed to have no other option. Lately I have thought a lot about where I am as a forty-four-year-old man. I don't know if it is a midlife crisis or a simple taking-stock, but I have definitely been thinking about how it is going. You get to a certain age, and you realize that this is your life. You will not run hurdles at the Olympics or live on a mountain in Switzerland. This is my wife and my family. This is my job and the rate at which I am going bald. Then you decide how you feel about it. I am generally thrilled with my life, but at the same time Leslie and I often wonder why certain aspects of our life and relationship are not easier. This movie explores some of those questions.

Why aren't Seth Rogen and Katherine Heigl in the movie?

I wanted to focus on Pete and Debbie. I am just as interested in what happened to Ben and Allison, but it seemed apparent that if they were in the movie a little bit, people would want more. So it was an all-or-nothing proposition. There is plenty of time to do that spin-off if an idea occurs to me. In my mind I thought that if the audience demanded to see them, I could shoot a funny Skype call where we see their child, now six, doing something outrageous with Ben as a kind of puppeteer hiding in the background. Luckily, the audience did not demand it. I knew that if the crowd didn't ask too much about Ben and Allison, I would know they were fully engaged with Pete and Debbie, and that is what happened.

Are more sequels coming?

There is a part of me that wants to make a sequel every seven years, like Michael Apted's *Seven Up* documentary series. I love television, so I want one hundred episodes of every movie I make. I always want to spend more time with characters that I care about. Where are the guys from *Superbad*? Seth and Jonah didn't want to ruin *Superbad* by risking a bad sequel, but I am always for taking that risk. If nobody did, then we wouldn't have *The Godfather: Part II*.

What is it like working with your family?

I love it. I love them and like to see them every day. They are also talented and attractive, so that helps. Leslie is the bravest actress I know. She can be heartbreaking and hilarious at the same time. Nobody can do that quite like her. She is constantly pushing me to be more truthful and to go deeper. Many of the ideas in this script came from our discussion about the film. Maude and Iris really make me laugh. They understand how to work in this fluid process in the same way Paul Rudd and Charlyne Yi do. They are little professionals who are not intimidated by a set because they have been on them for their entire lives. This is the first time they have had a lot to do, and real scenes to play. They made as big a contribution to the film as anyone. A lot of the story is about their arguments and sibling rivalry, but the great thing that happened when we shot is that they bonded and enjoyed working together. So the movie helped solve the problem the movie talks about.

What is next?

I don't know. I have written about high school, college, post-college, virginity, pregnancy, marriage, aging, and death. I may have no choice but to go supernatural. I have milked this life and now need to write about ghosts and goblins, or intergalactic creatures. The truth is that something will happen and I will realize that I have no choice but to write a movie about it in order to figure out how I feel about it. I hope it will be something good!

This is 40

by
Judd Apatow

INT. MASTER BATHROOM - DAY

PETE (39) and DEBBIE (39) are having fantastic sex in the
shower. Debbie moans loudly. Pete is strong and sure of
himself. In total control.

                    DEBBIE
          Oh Pete! Oh my god! This is crazy!

                    PETE
          Oh my god. So incredible. Want to
          know a secret? I took a Viagra.

                    DEBBIE
          What?

                    PETE
          I took a Viagra. Those things
          totally work. This is awesome. Why
          don't I use this every day?

                    DEBBIE
          What? What did you do? Wait. Stop.

Debbie gets out of the shower. Pete follows.

                    PETE
          What's the matter?

                    DEBBIE
          You just took a Viagra to have sex
          with me?

                    PETE
          I thought it would make it better.
          It was better. It takes some of the
          pressure off.

                    DEBBIE
          Because you can't get hard without
          a Viagra? Is it because you don't
          think I'm sexy?

                    PETE
          I thought you'd think it was fun
          for me to supersize it for once.

                    DEBBIE
          That is the worst birthday present
          you could ever give someone.

                    PETE
          I was just trying to go turbo for
          your birthday.
                         (MORE)

                    PETE (CONT'D)
My hard-ons are still in analog.
This shit's digital.

                    DEBBIE
I don't want a turbo penis. I like
your medium soft one.

                    PETE
Look, I can get it up. Just not
that far up.

                    DEBBIE
Where did you get this?

                    PETE
I got it from Barry.

                    DEBBIE
What? You got it from Barry?

                    PETE
Why do you care? This is my dick
we're talking about, not yours.

                    DEBBIE
We are young people. We don't need
medication to have sex.

                    PETE
I only took it because it's your
birthday. I thought you'd like it.
Happy fucking fortieth birthday.

                    DEBBIE
I am not forty! And I don't want to
have a husband who has to take
Viagra to get a hard-on.

                    PETE
I don't have to take it every time,
but once in a while...

                    DEBBIE
Fuck forty! Forty can suck my dick.

TITLE UP - THIS IS 40

INT. HALLWAY/SADIE'S ROOM - MORNING

Pete sneaks down the hallway. He kisses SADIE (13) as he
wakes her. She wants to be left alone.

                         SADIE
              Your breath smells weird.

Pete breathes all over her as he talks.

                         PETE
              Wake up, wake up. Time to get up.

INT. CHARLOTTE'S ROOM - MORNING

Pete lifts a sleeping CHARLOTTE (8) out of bed and walks her
downstairs. It looks ridiculous because she is too tall to
hold her like she is a baby.

INT. BREAKFAST NOOK - MORNING

Pete and the kids set up a tray of muffins and donuts on the
table and decorate the room with birthday balloons,
streamers, etc. Pete sneaks bacon, cupcakes, and mini donuts
into his mouth occasionally. The house is a bit more
cluttered and messier than when we last saw it in *Knocked Up*.

INT. MASTER BATHROOM - MORNING

Debbie opens a window and sneaks a cigarette.

                         PETE (O.C.)
              We're ready!

She holds her cigarette with a yellow dish washing glove. She
puts out the cigarette and goes through an elaborate routine
of hiding the smell of smoke. She puts some weird oil in her
hair and uses a wet nap on her neck and clothes and brushes
her teeth. She sprays cologne and walks through it.

INT. KITCHEN - MORNING

Pete and the kids hold a cake and sing "Happy Birthday" as
Debbie walks in. When they are done she blows out the candles
on the cake which says "Happy 38th Birthday."

                         PETE
              Make a wish!

INT. KITCHEN, TV AREA - MORNING

The kids eat cereal. Sadie watches *Lost* on her iPad while
Pete and Debbie talk in the kitchen.

                    CHARLOTTE
          Can I watch *Lost*?

                    SADIE
          You can't handle *Lost*. It's too
          violent, and you won't understand.

                    CHARLOTTE
          If I don't understand it, why can't
          I handle it?

                    SADIE
          Because you're eight.

                    CHARLOTTE
          I can handle it. I've seen a shark
          eat a guy on *Shark Week*.

                    SADIE
          Shark Week is fake.

                    CHARLOTTE
          No, it's not.

                    SADIE
          All of it is reenactments.

                    CHARLOTTE
          I know but they--

                    SADIE
          That's scary! You shouldn't be
          allowed to watch that.

                    CHARLOTTE
          --they show the reenactments but
          they actually happened.

                    SADIE
          It's going to give you nightmares.

                    CHARLOTTE
          I can handle a nightmare. You're a
          nightmare every day for me.

INT. KITCHEN - MORNING

Pete clears the breakfast dishes.

                    DEBBIE
          Hey. Don't eat that cupcake.

                    PETE
          What?

                    DEBBIE
          The one you just put into the sink.
          I saw you were hiding that.

                    PETE
          This cupcake? You think I'm going
          to eat this cupcake?

                    DEBBIE
          Yeah.

                    PETE
          I so don't want this cupcake. Look.

He turns on the faucet and pours water on the cupcake.

                    DEBBIE
          You're still going to eat it.

                    PETE
          I'm going to eat this cupcake?

                    DEBBIE
          Just put it in the trash.

                    PETE
          What would you like to do today?
          Your choice.

                    DEBBIE
          Anything?

                    PETE
          Yeah, anything.

                    DEBBIE
          Just hang out with you guys.

                    PETE
          Don't you want to get a massage? Or
          do something fun? Forty's huge.

                    DEBBIE
          I'm turning thirty-eight.

                    PETE
          Okay. Thirty-eight. We'll move on.
          Isn't it weird that our birthday is
          the same week and that we're going
          to have a party, and it's just for
          me?

                    DEBBIE
          No. I don't think it's weird at
          all. Because you're turning forty
          and I'm turning thirty-eight.

                    PETE
          Come on. Do you really want to be
          one of those ladies who's just so
          insecure about their age and they
          lie and then they've got to
          remember.

                    DEBBIE
          You don't get it. You don't
          understand how it works. I don't
          want to shop at old lady stores. I
          don't want to go to J. Jill and
          Chicos and Ann Taylor Loft. I'm not
          ready yet. I need two more years.

                    PETE
          That is so insane, it kind of makes
          sense.

                    DEBBIE
          What did you get me for my
          birthday?

                    PETE
          I thought you said that we
          shouldn't get each other gifts this
          year?

                    DEBBIE
          What do you mean? You're supposed
          to get me a surprise gift. This is
          a big birthday. I'm turning forty!

INT. CHARLOTTE'S ROOM - MORNING

Charlotte plays the theme from *The Office* on her keyboard.

                    SADIE (O.C.)
          Mom!!

INT. SADIE'S ROOM - CONTINUOUS

Sadie tears apart her closet looking for clothes.

                    SADIE
          Mom! Why can't I get new clothes?!
          Nothing fits me!! God damn it!!

INT. KITCHEN - MORNING

Debbie is in workout gear. Pete enters wearing a lycra outfit
with all sorts of logos on it. He is a complete bicycling
asshole.

> DEBBIE
> I am going to work out. I'll be
> back in about an hour.

> PETE
> Hey, did your father call to wish
> you a happy birthday?

> DEBBIE
> No. That's no surprise.

Debbie leaves. Pete picks the soaking wet cupcake out of the
sink and takes a bite.

EXT. SANTA MONICA STAIRS - DAY

Debbie runs up a long flight of stairs with her trainer
JASON. Her friend BARB trails behind.

> JASON
> Come on.

> BARB
> Coming.

> JASON
> You've got to keep up with us,
> sweetheart. That's why your body
> looks like your body and her body
> looks like her body. Before, after.
> Before, after.

> BARB
> You guys just go on without me. I'm
> just gonna... fuck.

EXT. BRENTWOOD - MORNING

We see Pete in a large group of bikers riding down San
Vicente. Pete's friend BARRY is part of the group.

> BARRY
> Hey, thanks for letting me join
> this team.

                    PETE
          It's not really a team, it's just a
          bunch of guys who get together and
          ride.

                    BARRY
          I know, I know.

A car makes a right turn in front of Pete, nearly hitting
him. Pete bangs on the back of the car.

                    PETE
          Bike lane, asshole! It's always the
          guy in the fucking Infiniti.

EXT. STREETS NEAR THE STAIRS - DAY

Debbie is doing sit-ups while talking to Jason, who holds her
feet down. In the background, Barb stretches on a yoga ball.

                    JASON
          So why on earth is Pete taking
          Viagra? What's going on?

                    DEBBIE
          I don't know. I think maybe he just
          isn't attracted to me anymore.

                    JASON
          That is ridiculous. If you were my
          girlfriend, I would not need a
          Viagra. I would need an anti-Viagra
          pill. To try not to get a boner.

                    DEBBIE
          But everyone gives you a boner.

                    JASON
          Don't sell yourself short like
          that. You give me a boner.
             (whispers)
          Barb doesn't give me a boner.

                    DEBBIE
          Maybe things are just getting
          stale. That's why maybe I work out
          really hard. Maybe he'll be able to
          get a boner again.

                    BARB
          Why do you need to have sex, Deb?
          Sex is the number one thing people
          fight about.
             (MORE)

                    BARB (CONT'D)
You stop having sex, there will be
no more fights. I am living proof.
I have no sex, and I am the
happiest I've ever been.

                    JASON
I knew it. I knew you were not
having sex. I can see it on your
face. It's all puckered and pained.

                    BARB
I'm enjoying our non-sex period,
that's all I'm saying.

                    JASON
Don't you miss it?

                    BARB
Well, I wouldn't know, because I
don't have any feeling down there
anymore. I have nerve damage from
my C-section so everything is just
kinda-

                    DEBBIE
She's numb down there.

                    BARB
I could sit down hard on a fire
hydrant, and I wouldn't even know
that I was sitting. I could get
stung by a hornet down there, and I
would not feel it. You could put
anything in there, and I would not
know what the object was. I used to
pee in a nice stream, and now it
just kind of goes like a shower
head.

                    JASON
That is the saddest thing I've ever
heard.

                    DEBBIE
I think you need a family. Don't
you want a family?

                    JASON
No, I think I want to Clooney it.

                    DEBBIE
Clooney it?

                    JASON
          Yup.

                    DEBBIE
          He doesn't seem happy.

                    JASON
          Yeah, he is.

                    DEBBIE
          No. He's lonely.

                    JASON
          No, he's not.

                    DEBBIE
          See, I think he has sad eyes.

                    JASON
          Aw, you sweet little thing. He's
          doing sad, lonely eyes. To get the
          next lady. I can do it too, watch.

Jason demonstrates.

                    DEBBIE
          I bet George Clooney is really
          lonely. Just him and his pig.

                    JASON
          You'd fuck him.

                    DEBBIE
          I wouldn't.

                    JASON
          So would you.

                    BARB
          I would. I wouldn't feel it but-

                    JASON
          You'd fuck him with your numb
          vagina. Yes, you would. Ocean's
          thirteen inches, that's what you'd
          find out.

                    DEBBIE
          Do you think?

INT. STARBUCKS - MOMENTS LATER

Pete and Barry eat frosted scones, happy to get some alone time to delay their return home.

                    BARRY
          I mean that was idiotic. You have
          to understand. That's like the one
          thing you don't do is tell her you
          used Viagra. I think that's even on
          the warning label.

                    PETE
          We're in one of those phases where
          everything the other person says
          just annoys the shit out of each
          other. All the time. It's a blast.

                    BARRY
          Don't worry about it. You just
          gotta ride that out.

                    PETE
          This sounds terrible but do you
          ever wonder what it would be like
          if, say, you were separated by
          something bigger, like death. Like
          her death?

                    BARRY
          I have given it a fair amount of
          thought.

                    PETE
          Not in a painful way. Just quietly
          slid into death. Like a gas leak.

                    BARRY
          Absolutely. It has got to be
          peaceful. I mean this is the mother
          of your children.

                    PETE
          I'd want it to be a peaceful --
          just like, drift, into a coma, from
          which she never awakens.

                    BARRY
          Then you move on. Then you're a
          widower.

                    PETE
          That's just it. People love
          widowers.

                    BARRY
          They love widowers. It's like the
          polar opposite of divorced guys.

                    PETE
          It's the best.

                    BARRY
          It's like, oh, that poor widower.
          You know. If I could only--

                    PETE
          Somehow...

                    BARRY
          ...make him happy.

                    PETE
          Somehow ease his pain.

                    BARRY
          ...cocksuck away his sadness.

INT. CAR - DAY

The family is driving. Sadie watches an episode of *Lost* on an
iPad. The Pixies play on the stereo, and Pete sings along.

                    PETE
          Did you know that the Pixies did
          this song about a Salvador Dali
          short film called "Un Chien
          Andalou"?

                    DEBBIE
          This music doesn't make people
          happy.

                    PETE
          This song kicks off *Doolittle*, one
          of the best albums of the last
          thirty years. An important record.

                    DEBBIE
          Look how angry you get while
          listening to this.
               (beat)
          It's my birthday. You don't control
          the radio on my birthday. I control
          the radio on my birthday.

Debbie switches the radio and sings along to "Take On Me" by
Ah-Hah.

Sadie stares at her iPad. We see a violent scene.

                    CHARLOTTE
          Sadie's watching *Lost*.

                    DEBBIE
          Sadie, how many times have you
          watched *Lost* this week?

                    SADIE
          I've only watched eleven. I have
          eight more and then I'm done.

                    PETE
          How many are there?

                    SADIE
          A hundred and fourteen?

                    PETE
          Are you kidding me? You can't watch
          over a hundred episodes of a show
          in five weeks. It'll melt your
          brain.

                    SADIE
          It's not melting my brain, it's
          blowing my mind.

                    DEBBIE
          That's really bad, Sadie. You're
          not allowed to do that.

                    SADIE
          My relationship with *Lost* is not
          your business. It's extremely
          personal.

Charlotte grabs for Sadie's iPad, then starts trying to lick
her.

                    SADIE (CONT'D)
          Stop it!

                    DEBBIE
          Be nice to your sister. You guys
          are going to cherish each other one
          day.

                    SADIE
          Stop it! Stop!

EXT. MONTANA AVENUE - DAY

Pete and Debbie get out of the car and walk down the street.

                    PETE
          It's your birthday, you don't need
          to go to the store.

                    DEBBIE
          I know, just five minutes. I think
          Desi and Jodi are fighting.

                    PETE
          All right, five minutes. But then
          I'm pulling you out.

INT. DEBBIE'S STORE - DAY

Pete and Debbie enter and we see their two employees, JODI
and a new, gorgeous employee, DESI, who is up on a ladder.

                    DEBBIE
          Hi. How's Jodi treating you?

                    DESI
          Jodi? Oh, Jodi's my new BFF. She's
          like a little kitty cat. Sometimes
          she comes and rubs up against my
          leg.

                    JODI
          You're a ball of shit.

                    DESI
          She loves me.

                    DEBBIE
          Huh.

Debbie goes behind the register. She looks at Jodi.

                    DEBBIE (CONT'D)
          Can you do inventory so that we can
          do the sidewalk sale? And you
          really need to pay attention to the
          numbers because we have twelve
          thousand dollars unaccounted for.

                    JODI
          I think it's probably Desi. She's
          been having a really hard time
          using these simple computers.
                    (MORE)

                    JODI (CONT'D)
It's because she's stupid. I think
she might be stealing.

                    DEBBIE
She's not stealing. She's our best
employee. She made nine grand last
month.

                    JODI
Well, how much did I make?

                    DEBBIE
You brought in twenty-two hundred.

                    JODI
That's not bad.

                    DEBBIE
Well, that's not that good. I mean,
I'm not comparing you, but you're
not as good.

Pete is still staring at Desi on the ladder.

                    PETE
              (to Desi)
All right. See you.

Pete walks over to Debbie.

                    PETE (CONT'D)
I don't think she's wearing
underwear.

                    DEBBIE
What?

                    PETE
It's all dark up there.

                    DEBBIE
What? Why are you looking?

                    PETE
I didn't mean to look, I just said,
'Hey- woah!' There it was.

                    DEBBIE
Maybe she's wearing dark underwear.

                    PETE
Yeah. Maybe she has underwear that
has a picture of a vagina painted
on it.

                         DEBBIE
              Stop looking.

Desi comes down to help a CUSTOMER at the front of the store.

                         DESI
              Maybe some deep oranges and browns
              and maybe dark greens? That would
              really play up your features.

                         CUSTOMER
              I'll just take out my AmEx and you
              pick what stuff you think is good.

EXT. BACKYARD - DAY

We see quick cuts of Debbie playing with the kids on the
trampoline outside. She does a full flip and lands on her
feet. Pete is nowhere to be found.

                         DEBBIE
              Woo! Where's daddy?

                         SADIE
              I think he went to poop.

                         DEBBIE
              Pete!

INT. HOUSE - CONTINUOUS

Debbie walks down the hall and into the bathroom without
knocking. Pete is on the toilet playing Scrabble on his iPad.

                         DEBBIE
              What are you doing?

                         PETE
              Going to the bathroom.

                         DEBBIE
              We're all downstairs waiting for
              you. You've been up here for a
              really long time now.

                         PETE
              Oh, I'm almost done. I'll be down
              in a second.

                    DEBBIE
Charlotte just did her first flip
on the trampoline, and she landed
on her feet. She was really proud
of herself.

                    PETE
Oh, that's great.

                    DEBBIE
And you missed it.

                    PETE
She'll do it again.

                    DEBBIE
It's just that this is the fourth
time you've gone to the bathroom
today.

                    PETE
Give me a break.

                    DEBBIE
Why is your instinct to escape?

                    PETE
It's not my instinct to escape from
you. It is my instinct to come into
the bathroom when I need to go to
the bathroom.

                    DEBBIE
How come I don't smell anything?

                    PETE
It's because I shoved an Altoid up
my ass before I came in here.

                    DEBBIE
Let me see then.

                    PETE
What?

                    DEBBIE
Let me see!

                    PETE
No, I'm not going to let you see.

                    DEBBIE
You're not going to let me see
because you're not taking a poop.

                    PETE
          I've been flushing as I go.

                    DEBBIE
          You're flushing as you go? Who
          takes a half hour to go to the
          bathroom?

                    PETE
               (thinks for a second)
          John Goodman.

She angrily grabs his iPad and walks out.

                    PETE (CONT'D)
          Don't press Enter! I'm not sure I
          want to make that move!

EXT. SMALL NIGHTCLUB - NIGHT

A sign outside reads: "Tonight Only: Graham Parker"

INT. SMALL NIGHTCLUB - STAGE - NIGHT

Pete stands on stage speaking to a small crowd.

                    PETE
          You know, when I started this
          label, my dream was to work with
          musicians and bands whose music I
          just admired so much. The person
          that I thought, "My god, wouldn't
          it be incredible to work with" was
          Graham Parker. Tonight we have him.
          Solo. Because we couldn't afford to
          fly in The Rumour.

The crowd applauds as Graham Parker (60's) leaps on stage.

Pete and Debbie watch Graham sing a very moving song. The
song is fantastic and personal, but clearly not commercial.

We watch Debbie. Although the music is great, it's a little
depressing and not working on her. She quickly gets bored.

INT. CAR - NIGHT

Pete and Debbie are driving home.

                    DEBBIE
          It's just not my kind of music.

                    PETE
          Really. What is your kind of music?

                    DEBBIE
          I like Lady Gaga.

                    PETE
          Oh, god, of course you do.

                    DEBBIE
          What?

                    PETE
          Shallow dance music.

                    DEBBIE
          It's not! It's fun, and it's about
          release and sex and power.

                    PETE
          You know, you don't have to like
          it. It's really not for you, that's
          fine.

                    DEBBIE
          This is a job. This is not a hobby.
          Can't you love him just as a hobby?
          And sign a fifteen-year-old hot
          girl so we can eat?

                    PETE
          Graham Parker and The Rumour had
          two albums in the *Rolling Stone* Top
          500 Best Albums of All Time. Two of
          'em. If I can just sell ten
          thousand records to his hardcore
          fan base, we're golden.

An ambulance drives by, sirens blaring.

                    DEBBIE
               (pause, then laughing)
          The last of Graham Parker's fans
          just died.

INT. SADIE'S ROOM - NIGHT

Pete and Debbie walk in mid-argument. Sadie is listening to a
song on her iPhone.

                    DEBBIE
          Sadie. Sadie, what are you
          listening to?
               (MORE)

                DEBBIE (CONT'D)
        Okay, this is music that makes
        people happy. And this is what
        people buy. Right, girls?

She puts Sadie's iPod in a dock and plays the Nikki Minaj rap
"Roman's Revenge." They all start rapping along to it.

They all laugh and dance and go crazy. Pete turns the iPod
off.

                DEBBIE (CONT'D)
        Why did you take it off?

                PETE
        Now, something that really rocks.

Pete puts on "Rooster" by Alice In Chains.

                PETE (CONT'D)
        This is called good music. From
        somebody's heart.

                SADIE
        This is bumming me out. This isn't
        fun.

                PETE
        Just listen to these words, okay?

                CHARLOTTE
        I don't understand the words.

                PETE
        This is lyrics, this is poetry.
        This is what is going to survive in
        a hundred years.

                DEBBIE
        It just doesn't make people happy.

                PETE
        It makes me happy. I can dance to
        it.

Pete starts dancing around like it is fun.

                DEBBIE
        You're the only one in the room
        who's happy.

Pete stops his music.

                    PETE
          Sometimes, I wish just one of you
          had a dick.

                    CHARLOTTE
          Well, we don't want one.

INT. HOUSE - MORNING

Pete sits with the kids and eats breakfast. Debbie scurries
around him to prep the kids for school.

                    DEBBIE
                 (to Pete)
          Is there something that you can do
          to be helping me right now?

                    PETE
          Yeah, I'm ready to help. Just tell
          me what to do.

                    DEBBIE
          Can you go get a lunch box or
          something?

                    PETE
          For me or for them?

Charlotte runs away towards her room. Sadie screams.

                    SADIE
          Charlotte! I've got a test!

                    CHARLOTTE
          I'm coming! I'm coming!

                    SADIE
          Charlotte, I'm going to kill you!

Debbie covers Sadie's mouth.

                    DEBBIE
          Shhh!

EXT. SCHOOL PARKING LOT - MORNING

Debbie drives the kids to school.

EXT. SCHOOL - MORNING

Debbie runs Charlotte into the school. Along the way they see
a lot of parents. Debbie says "Hi" to them in the way that
lets us know that she does not know anybody's name. Debbie
says "Hello" to a PREGNANT FIFTY-YEAR-OLD PARENT, towing a
seven-year-old boy.

                    DEBBIE
        Hi, any day now, huh?

                PREGNANT FIFTY-YEAR-OLD PARENT
        Not really. Three more months!

Another parent, BETH, and her adorable child walk over.

                    BETH
        Katie's dying for a play date.
        Let's hook these two up.

                    DEBBIE
        That would be great, I'll call you.

Beth and Katie walk off.

                  CHARLOTTE
    No.

                    DEBBIE
    "No" what?

                  CHARLOTTE
    No.

                    DEBBIE
    What? She's sweet.

                  CHARLOTTE
    She's evil.

INT./EXT. CHARLOTTE'S SCHOOL - MORNING

As they walk into class, the teacher pulls Debbie aside.

                    TEACHER
        Hi. Listen, Charlotte really needs
        to get here on time because she
        needs the extra time to just settle
        in.

                    DEBBIE
        Oh. We are on time.

                    TEACHER
          Being on time means being early.

                    DEBBIE
          Oh. Okay.

                    TEACHER
          Well, it's nice to see you in
          class. We'd like to see more of
          you.

                    DEBBIE
          I come to--

The teacher walks away before Debbie can defend herself.

                    GRANDMA MOLLY
          Hi Debbie!

                    DEBBIE
          Hi, Grandma Molly.

                    GRANDMA MOLLY
          How are you? I'm so happy about the
          science fair. It's going very well
          I heard. I love you. You look so
          beautiful. Happy birthday! I just
          learned it's your fortieth. Are you
          forty?

                    DEBBIE
          Yeah.

                    GRANDMA MOLLY
          I remember when I was forty, and
          then I blinked and there I was,
          going to be ninety. My god, where
          did it go? One day you're going to
          blink, and you're going to be
          ninety, and I won't be around to
          see it. And that makes me very sad.
          I'm telling you, I'm warning you.
          Don't blink. Don't blink.

EXT. SCHOOL PARKING LOT - DAY

As Debbie pulls out of the lot, she lights a cigarette.

INT. PETE'S MUSIC LABEL - DAY

Pete paces around his office on the phone.

                    ACCOUNTANT (O.C.)
And then you missed the mortgage
payment, and that's the second
mortgage. You've got to tighten
your belt. You've got to go home,
sit down, look at your expenses,
come clean with Debbie.

                    PETE
Oh, god. I can't tell Debbie.

                    ACCOUNTANT (O.C.)
You have to tell her, Pete.

                    PETE
She knows it's bad, but she has no
idea just how bad.

                    ACCOUNTANT (O.C.)
If you sell the house, it'll really
buy you some time.

                    PETE
No. Debbie's not really into
selling the house.

                    ACCOUNTANT (O.C.)
As your business manager and your
friend, I can't recommend that.
     (beat)
Hey, how funny would it be if I
bought your house?

                    PETE
Okay. Bye.

                    ACCOUNTANT (O.C)
Hang in there.

Pete is with RONNIE and CAT, employees at his record label.
They are watching an electronic press kit cut together for
Graham Parker. There is a montage of him performing
throughout the years from the seventies to the present.

                    RONNIE
What are you doing?

                    CAT
I'm contextualizing him as one of
the great figures in rock history.

                    RONNIE
You can't show him in his prime in
'77 and then jump straight to him
as he is now. It's terrifying. You
have to reverse it. You've got to
show him as he is now very briefly,
and then show him in 1977. You have
to "Benjamin Button" it.

                    CAT
I don't know what you're talking
about, okay? All rock stars are
older now. Steven Tyler, David
Bowie, Mick Jagger--

                    PETE
Paul McCartney.

                    RONNIE
Okay, stop it. Everybody you're
mentioning looks like an old woman
now. You're just mentioning a bunch
of Jessica Tandys. Keith Richards
gets away with it. But that's
because Keith Richards looked
seventy when he was forty, and now
that he's seventy, he looks sixty-
nine. He's regenerating.

                    CAT
I like it. And I think Graham
Parker is sexy.

                    RONNIE
Would you fuck him?

                    CAT
Yes.

                    RONNIE
You'd fuck him, and you won't fuck
me?

                    CAT
I mean, I kind of fucked you once,
if you could have finished.

                    RONNIE
Oh, I finished.

                    PETE
You know what, enough of who fucked
who and who finished what.

                    RONNIE
          I finished.

                    PETE
          Look. It's a retro label. That's
          our niche. That's our market. It
          costs money to break new bands, I
          can't do that.

                    RONNIE
          Oh, okay. And also you're the guy
          who turned down Arcade Fire.

                    PETE
          Everyone turned down Arcade Fire.

                    CAT
          It's crazy, there are so many of
          them!

                    PETE
          We don't have the money to market a
          new band. We just need to make
          Graham seem relevant. Who is he
          talking to?

                    CAT
          Um, the *Jewish Journal*.

                    PETE
          The *Jewish Journal*?

                    RONNIE
          Apparently old Jews are the only
          ones who still buy hard copies of
          records. Because they don't like to
          download music. Because they don't
          know what downloading means.

Angle on Graham and a journalist wearing a yarmulke.

                    INTERVIEWER
          Why is this album different from
          any other album?

                    GRAHAM
          It isn't.

Angle on Pete, Cat and Ronnie.

                    PETE
          What is he wearing?

                    CAT
It's a hat with the Oreo logo on
it.

                    PETE
Why?

                    CAT
I don't think he's being ironic, I
think he just really likes Oreos.

                    PETE
Look. The Paul Westerberg record
did okay. Frank Black did all
right. The Haircut 100, not so
much. We have to break this record.
Otherwise, we're not here next
year.

                    RONNIE
He's coming. Oreo man is coming.

Graham walks up.

                    GRAHAM
Hey guys, how are you?

                    RONNIE
Aren't cookies the best?

                    GRAHAM
Yeah. *Jewish Journal* guy loves the
record.

                    PETE
Great!

                    GRAHAM
Got a bit of a problem. Touch of
gout.

                    PETE
Gout?

                    GRAHAM
Yeah, my whole family, they all had
gout.

                    PETE
Jesus.

                    RONNIE
That's very unfortunate.

                    GRAHAM
          My auntie Queenie, she had a foot
          like the size of a small pig. I've
          got a photo of it.

                    RONNIE
          I'd love to see that photo of that
          gout foot.

                    GRAHAM
          A couple of bunions as well.

                    RONNIE
          Fuck.

                    GRAHAM
          I've got to go to the podiatrist,
          and I hope he can shoot me up with
          something.

                    PETE
          Yeah, well, let's get you to the
          podiatrist.

                    CAT
          Bye, Graham.

                    RONNIE
          See you later, Graham. Good luck
          with your gout!

                    GRAHAM
          Rock and Roll, baby.

INT. PETE'S HOME OFFICE - AFTERNOON

Pete and Debbie are talking. Debbie holds a list of changes
she wants to make.

                    DEBBIE
          The happiest period in people's
          lives is from age forty to sixty.
          So this is it. We're in it, right
          now.

                    PETE
          Says who?

                    DEBBIE
          Says a lot of people, most people.

                    PETE
          Huh.

                    DEBBIE
We have everything we need right
now to be completely happy. We're
going to blink and be ninety.

                    PETE
What?

                    DEBBIE
So, let's just choose to be happy.

                    PETE
Yeah.

                    DEBBIE
Your eyes are kind of glazing over.

                    PETE
No, I'm just processing it all.

                    DEBBIE
Some of these I wrote for you. So,
we have to exercise every day.
Spend more time alone together. We
have to go to the therapist every
week.

                    PETE
That's a little pricey.

                    DEBBIE
No stressing over tiny things.

                    PETE
Yeah, that's good. You should do
that.

                    DEBBIE
We have to get more involved in
school. Have more patience with the
kids. And we need to work on our
anger.

                    PETE
Yeah, I think it would be good if
you could take care of your anger.

                    DEBBIE
No, I said both of us.

                    PETE
That's what I said. Our anger.

                    DEBBIE
          Okay. No more smoking.

                    PETE
          Yeah, you've got to cut that out.

                    DEBBIE
          I don't want to make this about a
          fight, I want to just be positive.

                    PETE
          Sorry.

                    DEBBIE
          Okay, and then no more holding on
          to resentments. We have to just let
          that go.

                    PETE
          So, you're saying that if we're
          arguing and I apologize, you'll let
          it go and not throw it back in my
          face later?

                    DEBBIE
          Well, I don't do that, but I will
          continue not to do that. What did
          you write?

                    PETE
          All of that. That's plenty. That's
          a lot.

                    DEBBIE
          And you're going to eat better?

                    PETE
          Oh, yeah. I've been doing a decent
          job, but I don't think there's
          anything wrong with having some
          fries every now and again.

                    DEBBIE
          And then I'll smoke that day.

                    PETE
          That's not the same thing.

                    DEBBIE
          It is the same thing.

                    PETE
          I like fries.

                         DEBBIE
          And the other thing is your dad
          stuff.

Pete picks up a guitar and starts playing with it.

                         DEBBIE (CONT'D)
          The not letting him guilt trip you
          all the time, because that puts a
          lot of pressure on you, and the
          whole family feels it. He's a grown
          man, and he's not our
          responsibility. And you're not
          giving him money anymore, right?

                         PETE
          No, I haven't been giving him money
          for years, I told you.

                         DEBBIE
          Can you please put that down?

INT. BEDROOM - NIGHT

Pete and Debbie are in bed. Debbie has a computer on her lap.

                         DEBBIE
          A lot of people are RSVP-ing to
          your birthday party.

                         PETE
          You sure you don't want to just do
          a joint birthday party?

                         DEBBIE
          No.

                         PETE
          We always used to.

                         DEBBIE
          No.

We reveal that Debbie is watching security cam footage of the
store.

                         DEBBIE (CONT'D)
          Did Jodi tell you she thinks Desi's
          stealing?

                         PETE
          Are you serious?

                    DEBBIE
          Yes.

                    PETE
          How much?

                    DEBBIE
          Twelve thousand dollars.

                    PETE
          Oh, god. And Desi's taking it?

                    DEBBIE
          Well, I don't know. That's what
          Jodi said.

                    PETE
          We really need the store to work.

                    DEBBIE
          It is. Don't put that kind of
          pressure on me.

                    PETE
          That's not what I mean.

                    DEBBIE
          Are you nervous about money? Are we
          okay?

                    PETE
          Yeah. Maybe we just suck it up
          because she's clearly earning so
          much more than any other employee
          we have.

                    DEBBIE
          Oh, yeah. For sure. We can't fire
          her. We're barely breaking even
          with her.

                    PETE
          That's why we have to keep her.

We watch the footage and suddenly Desi's BOYFRIEND enters. He
walks behind the counter, and she sits on his lap. She
adjusts herself.

                    DEBBIE
          Look at this, she's making out with
          somebody.

On the screen, they kiss. Desi seems to be popping up and
down a little.

                    DEBBIE (CONT'D)
          Is she screwing him??

                    PETE
          That might be like a dry hump.

                    DEBBIE
          Look at the position of her skirt.

                    PETE
          That's too grainy to know for sure.
          Oh my god, this is the middle of
          the day. Customers could be in
          there.

                    DEBBIE
          At least she's getting some.

                    PETE
          What did you say? "At least she's
          getting some"?

                    DEBBIE
          Yes.

                    PETE
          What are you talking about? We had
          sex the other night. You have to
          give me a little credit for that.

                    DEBBIE
          It's not about credit. We need to
          have more passion. Like this.

                    PETE
          That's not passion.

                    DEBBIE
          It looks like passion to me.

                    PETE
          What--

Pete farts.

                    PETE (CONT'D)
          What is she doing?

He farts again. It is longer.

                    DEBBIE
          Oh my god. Don't do that!

Debbie hits Pete with a pillow.

                    PETE
          What am I doing?

                    DEBBIE
          Don't fart in the bed!

                    PETE
          I'm not, it's the springs.

                    DEBBIE
          This is why we never have sex.
          That's disgusting. You're gross.

                    PETE
          I don't know what you're talking
          about.

Pete farts again.

INT. SADIE'S ROOM - NIGHT

Charlotte jumps around in front of Sadie's door. Sadie sits
on her bed quietly doing homework.

                    CHARLOTTE
               (singing)
          Sadie. Sadie, Sadie! Sadie, Sadie!

                    SADIE
          Charlotte. I'm doing my homework.

                    CHARLOTTE
          Okay, watch this. There's a haunted
          cow back here, and I'm pretty sure
          it does not have milk!

Charlotte grabs her own head and makes it look like she's
being dragged away.

                    CHARLOTTE (CONT'D)
          Did you see that? They took me
          away!

Sadie does not even look up.

                    CHARLOTTE (CONT'D)
          You're no fun. You never want to
          play.

                    SADIE
          Charlotte. How many times do I have
          to tell you--

                    CHARLOTTE
                  (singing)
          Sadie! Sadie, Sadie! Is boring!

Charlotte plays air guitar. Sadie does not respond.

                    CHARLOTTE (CONT'D)
          You're so mean since your body got
          weird.

                    SADIE
          Close the door.

EXT. HOUSE - MORNING

Debbie and Pete begin their "fresh start." Debbie tosses her
cigarettes in the garbage cans outside. Pete tosses a packet
of M&M's in the garbage. He throws out all of his cupcakes
except for one. He takes a bite, tries to throw it but again,
can't. He takes another bite, holds it over the garbage, then
takes one last bite before dumping what little remains.

INT. DOCTOR'S OFFICE - DAY

Pete runs on a treadmill while getting an electrocardiogram.

INT. DOCTOR'S OFFICE - DAY

Debbie is getting a mammogram. The machine clamps too hard on
her breast. She screams.

INT. DOCTOR'S OFFICE- DAY

Pete gets his testicles examined.

                    DR. BOWE
          Did I tell you that my son is going
          to Stanford?

                    PETE
          No, that's great.

                    DR. BOWE
          Great for us and great for him.
          Cough again. Everything looks good.

                    PETE
          Your face is close to my face.

INT. DOCTOR'S OFFICE - DAY

Debbie is getting a colonoscopy.

                    TECHNICIAN
          Descending colon. I'm about four
          feet in right now.

                    DEBBIE
                (laughing)
          That's what he said.

INT. DENTIST OFFICE -DAY

Debbie has some sort of very painful oral surgery. She's a
little high from the laughing gas.

                    DENTIST
          Do you grind your teeth?

                    DEBBIE
          I grind all night.

                    DENTIST
          I think we need to turn the gas
          down.

                    DEBBIE
          Turn it up!

                    DENTIST
          No, we're going to turn it down.

                    DEBBIE
          Turn it up!

INT. DOCTOR'S OFFICE - DAY

Dr. Bowe has his finger inside of Pete's anus, giving him a
prostate exam.

                    PETE
          Do you have to breathe right on my
          neck?

                  DR. BOWE
          Sorry.

INT. GYNECOLOGIST OFFICE

Debbie is at the Gynecologist. He is the same one from the
beginning of *Knocked Up,* DR. PELLIGRINO. Debbie's legs are up
in stirrups.

                    DR. PELLIGRINO
          What are you all doing for
          Christmas?

                    DEBBIE
          I don't know.

                    DR. PELLIGRINO
          Do you have a tree and everything?

                    DEBBIE
          Yes.

                    DR. PELLIGRINO
          Isn't that fun. Get in the spirit--

Two nurses enter the exam room.

                    NURSE #1
          Hi, sorry I just have one quick
          question. On your form you said you
          were born in 1974, but your paper
          said 1972. I just need to know
          which it is.

                    DEBBIE
          Oh. It's 1974.

                    NURSE #2
          Because on your last form you said
          that you were born in 1975.

                    DR. PELLIGRINO
          Didn't you tell me you were born in
          1976?

                    DEBBIE
          No. That's funny.

                    NURSE #2
          So you want to go with 1974?

                    DEBBIE
          I'm not going to "go" with 1974, it
          is 1974.

                    NURSE #2
          Okay. Just remember to write 1974
          every time.

                    DR. PELLIGRINO
          It's okay. It's 1976.

                    DEBBIE
          I lie about my age, okay?

                    DR. PELLIGRINO
          Okay.

                    DEBBIE
          Okay? Okay? Okay?!

                    DR. PELLIGRINO
          You're tightening up.

                    DEBBIE
          Oh my gosh.

                    DR. PELLIGRINO
          I know how old you are. By counting
          the rings! Little gyno joke.

INT. BEDROOM - LATER

Debbie comes in the bedroom.

                    DEBBIE
          What are you doing?

                    PETE
          Getting ready to go for my ride.

                    DEBBIE
          You want a blow job?

                    PETE
          Yeah. Why?

                    DEBBIE
          I really want a cigarette right
          now.

                    PETE
          Well, happy to help.

INT. HALLWAY - CONTINUOUS

Sadie runs down the hallway.

                    SADIE
        Charlotte, where is my backpack?

INT. OUTSIDE THE BEDROOM - CONTINUOUS

Charlotte tries to open the door, it's locked.

INT. BEDROOM - CONTINUOUS

Debbie is giving Pete a blow job out of frame. Pete is
sitting on a chair, super happy.

                    CHARLOTTE (O.C.)
        Hello?

                    PETE
        Mom's busy!

                    CHARLOTTE (O.C.)
        Why are you locking the door? Mom!

INT. OUTSIDE THE BEDROOM - CONTINUOUS

                    CHARLOTTE
        What's going on in there?

                    SADIE
        Mom, I can't be late for school, I
        have a test!

                    PETE (O.C.)
        Mommy can't talk right now!

INT. BEDROOM - CONTINUOUS

                    SADIE (O.C.)
        This isn't funny, Mom. I need to
        go.

                    CHARLOTTE (O.C.)
        Mom, let me in!

INT. OUTSIDE THE BEDROOM - CONTINUOUS

                    SADIE
        That's not going to help.

Charlotte shoves Sadie.

                    PETE (O.C.)
          Put on your shoes. We'll meet you
          in the car.

The fight between Sadie and Charlotte escalates and becomes
physical.

INT. BEDROOM - CONTINUOUS

                    CHARLOTTE (O.C.)
          Sadie hurt me!

                    SADIE (O.C.)
          I didn't!

                    PETE
          Hit her back!

                    SADIE (O.C.)
          She's faking!

INT. OUTSIDE THE BEDROOM - CONTINUOUS

                    CHARLOTTE
               (crying)
          I'm not!

                    PETE (O.S.)
          Go downstairs.

INT. BEDROOM - CONTINUOUS

                    DEBBIE
               (shouting to kids)
          Stop crying!

                    PETE
               (to kids)
          Stop crying!

                    DEBBIE
          Stop it!

                    PETE
          God damn it!

INT. OUTSIDE THE BEDROOM - CONTINUOUS

> SADIE
> (banging on the door)
> Open the door! Open it!

INT. BEDROOM - CONTINUOUS

Muffled screams from the girls outside.

> DEBBIE
> Forget it.

> PETE
> No. Don't forget it. Don't forget
> it. Don't. Oh, god.

EXT. LARRY'S HOUSE - EL SEGUNDO - DAY

Pete walks to the front door. His father, LARRY, greets him.

> LARRY
> Hey, Boychik.

A low flying 747 lets us know he lives too close to the airport in a small house.

> LARRY (CONT'D)
> That's the eleven o'clock from
> London.
> (yells up at the plane)
> Drop something valuable, you shit.
> (back to Pete)
> How are you?

> PETE
> That's loud.

> LARRY
> Every eight minutes, buddy.

INT. LARRY'S HOUSE - DAY

Pete sits down and talks with Larry.

> LARRY
> You look pretty good. Your hair is
> different.

> PETE
> Yeah, I'm growing it out.

                    LARRY
          I'd get it cut.

                    TRIPLET #1
          Daddy, you never play with me.

                    LARRY
          I do but right now look who I'm
          talking to. It's your brother.

                    TRIPLET #1
          You don't look like my brother.

                    LARRY
          I told you honey, that's because of
          the egg donor. Remember?

                    TRIPLET #1
          I came from a test tube.

                    PETE
          How's business?

                    LARRY
          It's not good. Nobody wants
          curtains. They think of it like a
          luxury. It's not a luxury. You need
          shade, you need privacy. Who wants
          to have other people watch you
          fuck?

                    PETE
          I know how you feel. You know my
          business is going through some
          growing pains right now.

Two other identical children enter and jump on Larry.

                    TRIPLET #2
          Daddy come play with us.

The kids crawl around on him.

                    LARRY
          Be careful, don't jump on Daddy.
          Remember, Daddy has high blood
          what?

                    TRIPLETS
          Blood pressure.

                    LARRY
          That's right. Can you go outside
          without me for a little bit?
                    (MORE)

> LARRY (CONT'D)
> All right? Do the Three Stooges
> routine you were practicing.

The three exit.

> LARRY (CONT'D)
> I can't tell them apart. I swear to
> god. I need tattoos.

> PETE
> Look, I wanted to talk to you about
> scaling back a little bit. You
> know, Deb and I are thinking about
> selling the house.

> LARRY
> I think that house is more than you
> need. I think it was too big of a
> purchase when you made it.

> PETE
> Yeah. In the meantime, I'm going to
> have to make some changes. Going to
> have to cut back.

> LARRY
> What do you mean?

> PETE
> With you.

> LARRY
> Oh. I'm sorry, what?

> PETE
> I can't lend you any more money.

> LARRY
> No, that's a bad idea. That's not
> the way to cut back. I have three
> children, here.

> PETE
> What about Claire? Why can't she
> get a job?

> LARRY
> Claire takes care of your brothers.
> What do you want her to do? If she
> goes to work, then I've got to hire
> somebody.

                    PETE
          Well you've got to figure something
          out because I can't do it.

                    LARRY
          Okay, fine. Why don't we kill them?
          Come on, we'll kill two of them.
          I'll keep the best one. Really, it
          will save us both a lot of trouble.

Larry stands up and walks outside. Pete follows.

EXT. LARRY'S BACKYARD - CONTINUOUS

Larry prepares to spray the kids with the hose.

                    LARRY
          Line up! Line up for murder! Come
          on! Who wants to be killed?

                    TRIPLET #1
          I do!

                    LARRY
          Okay, we're eliminating one, we're
          cheaper already.

Larry sprays him with the hose.

                    TRIPLET #2
          Murder me!

                    LARRY
          Boom, dead. You're dead.

                    TRIPLET #2
          I'm dead!

                    LARRY
          All right, the kids are murdered.
          That will save us some money.

                    PETE
          Why would you have three kids,
          anyway? I mean, you're sixty years
          old. You have no money.

                    LARRY
          Because Claire wanted a baby. If we
          didn't at least try, she would have
          left me. She was forty-five years
          old. Nobody thought it would take.
                    (MORE)

                    LARRY (CONT'D)
The doctor when we were doing in
vitro was winking at me like,
"Don't worry, don't worry." We were
very unlucky. And now we have these
three beautiful children... Come
on, I've got to tell you something.

INT. LARRY'S HOUSE - MOMENTS LATER

                    PETE
What?

                    LARRY
Your mother wanted you aborted.

                    PETE
Oh, Jesus Christ.

                    LARRY
It's the truth. It was the
seventies. We were twenty-two years
old. That's what everybody did. You
did some blow, had sex, had an
abortion.

                    PETE
Really.

                    LARRY
Yes. We were on the way to the
doctor's office. I said, "Let's
stop, have a pizza, talk about it,
if you still want to do it after
lunch, it's okay." The pizza saved
your life. But don't give me money.
Because I'm not worth it.

                    PETE
So how much do I owe you for saving
my life?

                    LARRY
I don't have a number. You just
keep giving like you're giving.

Larry's wife, CLAIRE, enters.

                    CLAIRE
Oh, hi Pete.
     (to Larry)
Why aren't you playing with kids?

> LARRY
> We were playing with them all day.
> Pete's just talking to me about his
> fortieth birthday party... Whatever
> I can do to help.

> CLAIRE
> Okay. Did you feed them?

> LARRY
> I fed half of one. Okay, let's feed
> them. Who wants tuna with a side of
> jet fuel?

Larry gets up and walks outside.

INT. RESTAURANT - DAY

A nervous Debbie approaches a hostess.

> DEBBIE
> Hi, I'm looking for my dad, an
> older man?

Debbie sees OLIVER (65) sitting stiffly at a table.

INT. RESTAURANT - LATER

> OLIVER
> So how's Sony treating Pete?

> DEBBIE
> Oh, he's not with Sony anymore. He
> went out on his own. Now he's able
> to focus on the artists that he's
> really passionate about.

> OLIVER
> How's Sadie doing? Last time I saw
> her she was throwing her Cheerios
> on the floor. What a mess.

> DEBBIE
> She just got her period.

> OLIVER
> Well. I guess she's not a little
> baby anymore.

> DEBBIE
> It would be nice to see more of
> each other.

>   OLIVER
>   Well, we can certainly arrange for
>   that. I'd love to see the girls.

>   DEBBIE
>   That would be nice. Do you have a
>   good day?

>   OLIVER
>   I would say the weekends, but our
>   weekends are hell. Soccer
>   competitions, kids exams. I mean,
>   we're both so busy. I have young
>   children, you have young children.
>   I don't think we should judge
>   ourselves too harshly about that.

>   DEBBIE
>   I know, I wasn't. I'm glad we're
>   here. I think this is a good start
>   and that if we can spend more time
>   together, it would be nice.

>   OLIVER
>   It would be nice.
>   (pause)
>   Do you want to see pictures of the
>   kids?

Oliver takes out his iPhone and starts showing Debbie photos.

>   OLIVER (CONT'D)
>   This is Kell, my son.

>   DEBBIE
>   He's handsome. He's thirteen?

>   OLIVER
>   Yeah. And that's Alexandra, my
>   daughter, she's a real
>   perfectionist. A lot like you.
>   That's the whole gang at Cabo.
>   (pause)
>   Will you excuse me, dear? I've got
>   to use the restroom. Be right back.

He exits. Debbie picks up his iPhone and sadly scrolls
through all the happy pictures of his new family.

EXT. HOUSE - LATE AFTERNOON

The family's hanging out, relaxing at dinner.

                    DEBBIE
          Daddy and I are making some changes
          so that we can be happier and
          healthier, and we're starting with
          this meal that I prepared.

                    PETE
          I think it looks great.

                    DEBBIE
          Doesn't it look good?

                    PETE
          What is that, grilled cheeses?

                    DEBBIE
          No, baked tofu. It's actually
          really tasty. And the lettuce is so
          fresh and tasty that you forget how
          good lettuce tastes on its own
          without dressing.

                    PETE
          Yeah, dressing always gets in the
          way of the natural taste of the
          lettuce.

                    DEBBIE
          And another thing we've decided is
          to cut back on all of the
          electronics we use. What we're
          going to do is get rid of the wi-fi
          and only use the computer from
          eight to eight-thirty at night.

                    SADIE
          How are we going to go on the
          computer?

                    DEBBIE
          We're going to have a hard line in
          the kitchen.

                    PETE
          Yeah, we'll supervise that.

                    SADIE
          You can't do this. You can't take
          away the wi-fi.

Charlotte holds her iPhone to her face using an app that
animates her mouth to look like a talking monkey's.

                    CHARLOTTE
            (from behind her iPhone)
No wi-fi! Ha-ha-ha!

                    DEBBIE
You don't spend enough time with
the family when you're constantly
on your iPhone and your computer.
You're only here five more years.

                    SADIE
So you won't see me after five
years?

                    DEBBIE
No, but you won't be living with
us. And you should get to know your
little sister.

                    PETE
You've got the perfect friend right
here.

                    SADIE
I don't want to be friends with her
now. I'll be friends with her when
she's twenty and a normal person.

                    CHARLOTTE
I don't want to hang out with her
when I'm in my twenties.

                    PETE
You're on your computer too much as
it is. You need to get outside
more.

                    DEBBIE
Yeah. You can build things. You can
build a fort.

                    SADIE
What?

                    DEBBIE
Yeah, build a fort. Play with your
friends.

                    SADIE
Make a fort?! Outside? And do what
in the fort?

                    DEBBIE
          When I was a kid we used to build
          tree houses and play with sticks.

                    SADIE
          Nobody plays with sticks.

                    PETE
          You and Charlotte can have a
          lemonade stand.

                    DEBBIE
          Play Kick the Can.

                    PETE
          Look for dead bodies.

                    DEBBIE
          It's fun.

                    PETE
          Get a tire and then take a stick
          and run down the street with it.

                    SADIE
          Nobody does that crap. It's 2012.

                    DEBBIE
          You don't need technology.

Charlotte holds the iPhone monkey app to her lips again.

                    CHARLOTTE
          No technology!

                    DEBBIE
          Charlotte, put that down.

                    SADIE
          I don't need to be monitored all
          the time on the computer. I don't
          do anything bad.

                    DEBBIE
          Nobody said you were bad.

                    SADIE
          I don't do things I'm not supposed
          to. I don't illegally download
          music. I don't look at porn like
          Wendy.

                        DEBBIE
          She is up to no good. She's not
          allowed to come over here anymore.

                        CHARLOTTE
          What's porn?

                        PETE
          No, she said "corn."

                        DEBBIE
          This isn't turning out the way I
          wanted it to.

                        SADIE
          I'm not hungry.

Sadie gets up and stomps off.

                        DEBBIE
          No computer.

                        PETE
          Listen to your mom.

                        SADIE
          I need to use it for my homework.

She walks off.

                        PETE
          She's outplaying us.

                        DEBBIE
          I know. She's tough.

EXT. PETE AND DEBBIE'S CAR - DAY

Pete and Debbie drive down the Pacific Coast Highway.

                        DEBBIE
          This is the best birthday present.

                        PETE
          It's good to get away, you know? We
          haven't been to Laguna without the
          kids in years.

INT. PETE AND DEBBIE'S CAR - CONTINUOUS

                        DEBBIE
          I know!

                    PETE
          If we're happy, they're happy.

                    DEBBIE
          I mean I can't take it. With the
          hormones, and the crying, and "do
          my homework"...

                    PETE
          Them's little bitches.

                    DEBBIE
          Them's lil' bitches! Bugging us for
          shit all the time. And they never
          appreciate anything.

                    PETE
          God no. They're selfish assholes.

                    DEBBIE
             (laughs)
          Aw, I feel bad. I love them.

                    PETE
          I know.

EXT. LAGUNA HOTEL - CONTINUOUS

The car pulls up to a beautiful hotel in Laguna.

                    DEBBIE
          I miss them already. Should we go
          home?

                    PETE
          Nah.

LAGUNA HOTEL - MONTAGE

Pete and Debbie hold hands as they walk the hotel grounds.

They enter their room, which has a beautiful ocean view.
Debbie jumps on the bed. Pete jumps on top to kiss her.

Pete and Debbie jump into the hotel pool together.

Pete holds Debbie in the water. They kiss.

INT. LAGUNA HOTEL ROOM - NIGHT

Pete and Debbie are in bed in their underwear.

                    DEBBIE
Why do we fight?

                    PETE
I don't know, it makes no sense at
all.

                    DEBBIE
It makes no sense.

                    PETE
When we get in a fight, look in my
eyes. Let's remember this moment
right now and know that we never
have to fight.

                    DEBBIE
But you're such a dick sometimes.

                    PETE
I know, I am a dick sometimes.
People think I'm so nice, but I'm
such a dick.

                    DEBBIE
Thank you for admitting that.

                    PETE
And you get so mad at me. I feel
like you want to kill me.

                    DEBBIE
I do want to kill you.

                    PETE
How would you do it?

                    DEBBIE
I don't know... poison you. I'd
poison your cupcakes that you
pretend not to eat everyday. And
just put enough in to slowly weaken
you.

                    PETE
I love it.

                    DEBBIE
I would enjoy our last few months
together.

                    PETE
Me too.

                    DEBBIE
          Because you'd be so weak and sweet,
          and I could take care of you but
          while killing you.

                    PETE
          See? You know what I love about us?
          You can still surprise me. I
          figured for sure you'd knock me out
          with one fell swoop. But you would
          extend it over a series of months.

                    DEBBIE
          Have you ever thought about killing
          me?

                    PETE
          Oh, yeah.

                    DEBBIE
          Really?

                    PETE
          Sure.

                    DEBBIE
          How would you do it?

                    PETE
          Wood chipper.

                    DEBBIE
          A wood chipper?

                    PETE
          Did you see *Fargo*?

                    DEBBIE
          Yeah.

          Pete makes a wood chipping splatter noise.

                    DEBBIE (CONT'D)
          Wow. That's a bad plan. The
          cupcakes is a way better plan.

                    PETE
          It is. You know what? I won't
          murder you.

                    DEBBIE
          Aw. I love you.

                    PETE
          I love you too... Hey. You know
          what I brought?

                    DEBBIE
          What?

                    PETE
          A medical marijuana cookie. Ben
          gave it to me last Christmas.

                    DEBBIE
          What?

                    PETE
          Chocolate chip koo-kie.

                    DEBBIE
          Should we do it?

                    PETE
          Let's eat the cookie, and then
          we'll order a bunch of
          cheeseburgers. Let's order the
          entire room service menu.

                    DEBBIE
          Just get all of it. You deserve it.
          You really do.

                    PETE
          Wouldn't you rather have me around
          for less years and I'm incredibly
          happy than longer and miserable?

                    DEBBIE
          Yes, and I just realized that right
          now. Go get the cookie!

Pete runs into the bathroom. He looks for the cookie.

                    DEBBIE (CONT'D)
          Should we watch porn when we eat
          the cookie?

                    PETE
          Should we get a block of porn?

                    DEBBIE
          I don't think we need twenty-four
          hours of porn.

> PETE
> Yeah, but you know, two porns cost
> about as much as a block.

> DEBBIE
> I think that's too much porn.

> PETE
> We don't have to watch it all, but
> for the value it makes sense.

INT. HOTEL ROOM - LATER

Pete and Debbie eat the cookie.

> DEBBIE
> How much are we supposed to eat?

> PETE
> I don't know. I think like six or
> seven cookies, right?

> DEBBIE
> Plus, it's old. It probably has
> lost some of its-

> PETE
> Potency?

They sit in silence for an incredibly long amount of time,
staring through each other in a haze. They are stoned.

> DEBBIE
> We should have sex. More.

> PETE
> I mean, girls have it so easy. You
> just show up with your sexual
> organs and you're good to go. All
> the pressure is on the guy.

> DEBBIE
> It's true.

> PETE
> And I look at guys, like I look at
> a guy like Prince, and you know
> that guy fucks. I know I don't fuck
> like Prince. Prince can fuck. I
> fuck more like David Schwimmer.

> DEBBIE
> You do.

                    PETE
          I fuck like Ross from *Friends*.

They're laughing and having a good time.

INT. HOTEL ROOM - LATER

MONTAGE

Stoned, Pete and Debbie jump up and down on the bed.

They fall down on the bed, kissing.

Almost totally under the covers, they watch as a WAITER
brings in a room service cart full of food.

Pete does magic tricks for the waiter.

                    PETE
          How does he do it? The floating
          spoon.

LATER

Debbie hands Pete a banana and two oranges, which he holds to
his crotch in front of the waiter.

                    PETE (CONT'D)
          Check it out. My dick and balls.
          I'm going to eat my own dick!

Pete eats a bite of the banana.

                    PETE (CONT'D)
          I ate my dick!

LATER

Debbie crawls on the floor while Pete lays in bed.

                    PETE (CONT'D)
          I think this room has rodents. I
          just saw it!

LATER

Pete stands with a starfish sticking out of his underwear.

                    PETE (CONT'D)
          Have you seen my starfish? Where
          did I put my starfish?

LATER

They eat room service. Chips and desserts and everything.

>   DEBBIE
> I'm going to deep throat this
> eclair.

She tries to deep throat it. Pete loves it.

>   PETE
> I want to make out with you so bad.

INT./EXT. CAR - DAY

Pete and Debbie drive back from Laguna. They could not look happier or more refreshed. They hold hands and smile at each other. It is a beautiful day.

They pull up to their house, shut off the car and sit for a beat, knowing they're about to head back into the stress of the real world, not wanting their peaceful, loving time to end.

>   PETE
> That was nice.

>   DEBBIE
> That was nice.

Sadie walks outside. Jodi follows her.

>   SADIE
> Mom! Charlotte's crying. She's got
> an ear infection again.

>   JODI
> I didn't know what to do.

>   PETE
>   (to Debbie)
> We're home.

INT. CHARLOTTE'S ROOM - DAY

Charlotte is crying really hard.

>   DEBBIE
> Are you okay? What's the matter?

>   CHARLOTTE
> I just want to rip my ear off, it
> hurts so much.

                    DEBBIE
              (to Pete)
     I told you the pediatrician didn't
     know what he was talking about.

                    PETE
     Oh, come on. You can't blame it on
     our doctor. Ear infections are
     common in little kids.

                    DEBBIE
     Not in kids over six years old.
     We're going to the Eastern doctor.

                    PETE
     If she's in this much pain, we
     should call a real doctor.

                    DEBBIE
     Are you kidding right now?

                    PETE
     Okay.

INT. DOCTOR SEDUKU - DAY

Charlotte sits on the table. Pete and Debbie are talking to
DR. SEDUKU, a foreign doctor.

                    DOCTOR SEDUKU
     What we should do is easy and
     simple. No more dairy, no more
     wheat, no more sugar.

                    DEBBIE
     Sugar, wheat and dairy. Okay.

                    PETE
              (mutters)
     What the fuck is left? Sorry. Isn't
     everything sugar, wheat and dairy?

                    DOCTOR SEDUKU
     She can have vegetables and
     f-r-ruits.

Dr. Seduku has both an accent and a lisp.

                    PETE
     Oh, she can eat fr-r-ruits.

                    DOCTOR SEDUKU
     Fr-r-ruits, yes.

                    PETE
          Any kind of fr-r-ruits?

                    DOCTOR SEDUKU
          Mangos, pineapple...

                    PETE
          It isn't like there are safe fr-r-
          ruits and then unsafe fr-r-ruits.

                    DOCTOR SEDUKU
          No, no.

                    PETE
          What about F-r-r-rench f-r-r-ries?
          Can we do something like that?

                    DOCTOR SEDUKU
          Are you okay? Would you like to
          come on the table?

                    PETE
          I'm okay.

                    DEBBIE
          Why don't you go on the table?

                    PETE
          No.

                    DEBBIE
          Why don't you go on the table? It
          looks like you need to get on the
          table.

                    PETE
          I don't want to get on the table.

EXT. BRENTWOOD - DAY

Pete cycles with the crew.

INT. HOUSE - DAY - LATER

Debbie looks around the house for Pete.

                    DEBBIE
               Pete!

INT. BEDROOM - DAY

Debbie sees Pete on the bed, his legs up in the air. He still has his bike top on but is naked from the waist down.

He is trying to look at his back end. He is holding a mirror and an iPhone.

                    DEBBIE
          What are you doing?

                    PETE
          I need you to look at something. In
          my butt.

                    DEBBIE
          Why?

                    PETE
          I think I've got something in
          there, and I'm not limber enough to
          see. I need you to look at it. I
          might have like an anal fissure or
          a hemorrhoid or a worm or
          something.

                    DEBBIE
          What are you doing with your phone?

                    PETE
          Trying to take pictures of it, so I
          can compare it to something on
          Google.

                    DEBBIE
          Can we just keep like a small shred
          of mystery in our relationship?

                    PETE
          Look, I saw you have two babies,
          okay? Seriously, I need you to get
          all up in that.

                    DEBBIE
          I do not want to investigate your
          anus.

                    PETE
          It's payback time.

Pete has his naked legs hiked up over his head. Debbie takes a very quick glance inside.

                    DEBBIE
          It's a hemorrhoid.

                    PETE
          Thank you. Now erase that from your
          memory.

INT. DEBBIE'S STORE - DAY

Debbie talks to Jodi while they fold clothes and watch Desi.

                    DEBBIE
          Where did she get those clothes?
          Those are expensive.

                    JODI
          Where do you think? I don't want
          this to sound harsh, but everything
          that comes out of her mouth is a
          lie. Everything that comes into it
          is a dick.

                    DEBBIE
          Everything that goes in is dicks?

                    JODI
          A dick.

                    DEBBIE
          Don't say that.

                    JODI
          I'm sorry, I'm just being
          protective of the store.

                    DEBBIE
          I'm going to go talk to her.

Debbie walks over to Desi.

                    DEBBIE (CONT'D)
          Hey Desi. Is that your new Acura
          out front?

                    DESI
          Uh, yeah.

                    DEBBIE
          It's so nice. Do you love it?

                    DESI
          Well, I mean, it's not a fucking
          Porsche, but it'll do for now.

                    DEBBIE
          Hey Desi, would you mind wearing
          some of the clothes we have in the
          store?

                    DESI
          Yeah, sure. I'm sorry.

Desi picks a shirt.

                    DESI (CONT'D)
          Good?

Desi begins to take all her clothes off in front of Debbie.

                    DESI (CONT'D)
          You know, I actually made this one
          myself.

                    DEBBIE
          Did you?

                    DESI
          Yeah. I did the tiger on a piece of
          paper separately, and then I
          transferred it to the t-shirt.

                    DEBBIE
          Wow. So you stenciled on the tiger?

                    DESI
          I drew it on a piece of paper, and
          then I transferred the drawing to
          the t-shirt.

                    DEBBIE
          You have an amazing body.

                    DESI
          Really?

                    DEBBIE
          Yes. Are those real?

                    DESI
          My boobs? Yeah... Do you want to
          touch them?

                    DEBBIE
          Really?

                    DESI
          Touch 'em!

                    DEBBIE
          Okay.

Debbie squeezes Desi's breasts.

                    DEBBIE (CONT'D)
          Wow. Jesus. I mean they really are
          amazing. That's firm, for real.
          They're like a memory mattress.
          Like Tempurpedic, you know? They
          look amazing. My kids just sucked
          the meat right out of mine.

                    DESI
          No. There's some meat in there.

                    DEBBIE
          Since I had kids, my boobs are just
          gone. They didn't even say goodbye.
          They just left.

                    DESI
          By the time I'm forty, these are
          going to go National Geographic on
          me.

                    DEBBIE
          I feel bad about myself right now.

INT. RECORD LABEL - DAY

Pete talks is in his office on the phone with his REALTOR.

                    REALTOR (O.C.)
          I think this is a really good offer
          on the house.

                    PETE
          We expected more. I mean, I know
          it's a bad market but that's still
          way under what we were looking for.

                    REALTOR (O.C.)
          I know, but based on the market,
          it's like you're gaining money.
          Because it's so much more than what
          you deserve. But these people are
          from Iran and they don't really
          know that they're offering too
          much. Is there any chance that
          Debbie will go for it?

>   PETE
>   I doubt it. I don't know.
>
>   REALTOR (O.C.)
>   There's a lot of inventory out
>   there. What's her problem?
>
>   PETE
>   She has unrealistic expectations.

EXT. YARD - DAY

Sadie and her friend WENDY run around the yard with Charlotte and the triplets.

INT. KITCHEN PANTRY - DAY

Larry and Debbie greet the kids when they enter the kitchen. Larry picks up one of the triplets.

>   LARRY
>   Did you miss me Travis?
>
>   TRIPLET #1
>   It's Jack!
>
>   LARRY
>   Hey, Jack.
>
>   TRIPLET #1
>   My daddy doesn't know my name.
>
>   CHARLOTTE
>   Can I go show them my crystals
>   before they leave?
>
>   DEBBIE
>   Yeah, really quick.

Charlotte leaves with the triplets.

>   LARRY
>   Go play with your tiny uncles.
>   (to Debbie)
>   So, what are you doing, spring
>   cleaning?
>
>   DEBBIE
>   I'm getting rid of everything in
>   the house that has gluten or sugar.

LARRY
Why? What's wrong with gluten?

DEBBIE
Gluten's really bad for you.

LARRY
I don't think so. It's wheat.

DEBBIE
Don't you watch *Dr. Oz*?

LARRY
As in the *Wizard of*?

SADIE
Hey, Mom. We were wondering if we
could use the computer to iChat.

DEBBIE
Remember the rules? Eight to eight-
thirty?

SADIE
Yeah, but I have a friend over.

DEBBIE
Hi Wendy. Why don't you guys go
play? You could go build a fort!

LARRY
Remember the Alamo?

DEBBIE
Have you ever built a fort, Wendy?

WENDY
Like on Facebook?

LARRY
I will take this if you're going to
throw it away, because at our
house, we're wheat eaters.

DEBBIE
But don't you want to live long
enough to see your kids grow up?

LARRY
That's up to god, honey.

DEBBIE
But that's really not good for the
kids.

                    LARRY
          The kids eat grass. This is fine.

Larry takes some of the food she's throwing out.

                    SADIE
          Wendy's mom lets her go on whenever
          she wants.

                    WENDY
          My mom's pretty cool about it as
          long as I finish my homework.

                    DEBBIE
          Yeah. Well, I guess I'm not the
          cool one. But the rules are just
          different in our house.

                    SADIE
          But I get better grades than Wendy.

                    WENDY
          She does. She's so smart.

                    LARRY
          Let me just grab the candy worms.

                    SADIE
          Your rules are ridiculous.

                    DEBBIE
          Don't sass me.

                    SADIE
          I'm only sassing you because you're
          throwing out all the food in our
          house and I'm freaking starving.
          You're being stupid.

                    DEBBIE
          Wendy, can you go stand in the
          other room, please?

                    WENDY
          Yeah.

Wendy exits.

                    SADIE
               (whispers)
          Mom.

                    DEBBIE
          Give me your iPhone now.

                    LARRY
          The nougat things are good.

                    SADIE
          I have all my contacts in there.

                    DEBBIE
          Okay, if you don't give me your
          phone right now, then I'm going to
          have to take away your phone and
          your computer.

                    SADIE
          Jesus Christ--

                    DEBBIE
          That's it.

                    SADIE
          I need my computer to do homework.

                    DEBBIE
          No phone, no computer.

                    SADIE
          This is B.S. This is a bunch of F-
          ing S. You're acting like a B.

                    LARRY
          Kids! Time to go!

                    DEBBIE
          You go to your room right now.

Sadie runs off.

                    DEBBIE (CONT'D)
                (calling after her)
          You are not allowed to use iPhone,
          iPad, iPod Touch, iTunes, Netflix,
          Pandora, or Spotify!

Pete enters from the hallway. He sees Larry and turns around
before anyone notices him.

                    LARRY
          She's a little pip. Just like her
          mommy. So I might have a job
          tomorrow, at least I'm going to go
          try to give an estimate. Do you
          mind taking the kids for a couple
          hours?

                    DEBBIE
              (conflicted)
          Okay.

                    LARRY
          This is nice. You and I don't spend
          enough time together, do we?

                    DEBBIE
          We spend enough time together.

                    LARRY
          We do?

                    DEBBIE
          It's quality time.

                    LARRY
          Then we do. I'll go with what you
          think.

INT. BEDROOM - NIGHT

Pete and Debbie are in bed. Pete is reading Sadie's iChats on
her confiscated iPad out loud to Debbie.

                    DEBBIE
          What else did they say?

                    PETE
          Some kid named Joseph--

                    DEBBIE
          I know Joseph.

                    PETE
          You do? He's making a "Hot or Not"
          list.

                    DEBBIE
          What?

                    PETE
          So, Sadie said, "That's so lame and
          immature that you're doing that."
          And then Joseph says, "Yo, girl.
          We're just having some fun so don't
          be a bitch, yo."

                    DEBBIE
          That is not nice.

                    PETE
So, then Sadie said, "Don't call me
a bitch." And Joseph said, "I
didn't call you a bitch, I said
don't act like a bitch. And by the
way you're in the 'Not Hot'
column."

                    DEBBIE
Who made him the judge of hot?

                    PETE
Do you realize what that could do
to her self-esteem?

                    DEBBIE
What a little fuckhead. I'll kill
him.

                    PETE
So then Sadie said, "You're in the
jackass column. I've got to go. I'm
bored of you."

                    DEBBIE
That is cool. That's taking the
high road.

                    PETE
For some reason, there's an
emoticon of a panda doing push-ups.

                    DEBBIE
I wonder what that means.

                    PETE
I don't think it means anything, I
think it's just adorable.

                    DEBBIE
Aww. She's a good girl. She was
polite, and she stood up for
herself.

                    PETE
That's pretty cool.

They hear a door slam. Debbie gasps.

                    PETE (CONT'D)
What?

                    DEBBIE
Shit. I thought she was coming in.

> PETE
> Oh my god, that scared me to death.

> DEBBIE
> If she caught us, she would kill
> us.

Debbie starts looking through the iPad. Pete's iPhone chimes. He sees a message from Ronnie from work. It reads: "Got the numbers. Call me."

Pete looks ashen. He looks over at Debbie who is oblivious.

> PETE
> I've got to make a call.

INT. HOME OFFICE - NIGHT

Pete paces.

> PETE
> (whispering loudly)
> We sold how many?

> RONNIE (O.C.)
> Six hundred and twelve album
> downloads.

> PETE
> Wait a minute. There are no zeros
> after that?

> RONNIE (O.C.)
> There are zeros, but all of them
> are before six hundred and twelve.
> There are none after.

> PETE
> How is that even possible?

> RONNIE (O.C.)
> Out of three hundred million
> Americans, six hundred and twelve
> people chose to download the album.
> You could personally call everyone
> who bought this record.

> PETE
> We're fucked! Here's the deal. I
> want you to meet me tomorrow
> morning at eight o'clock. I want a
> list of at least thirty ideas of
> what we can do to change this.
> (MORE)

                    PETE (CONT'D)
          We have to change this. I started a
          record label because I couldn't get
          a job, so I have no other options.

INT. CAR - MORNING

Pete is driving. Sadie and Charlotte sing show tunes loudly
and happily. Pete is very upset about the record not selling.

INT. ACCOUNTANT'S OFFICE - DAY

Debbie is talking to their ACCOUNTANT.

                    DEBBIE
          What financial problems?

                    ACCOUNTANT
          Well, for one thing, you were
          right, you are missing about ten
          thousand dollars from the store.
          And then, Pete's record not selling
          well.

                    DEBBIE
          I thought we weren't supposed to
          hear for three weeks?

                    ACCOUNTANT
          We heard.

                    DEBBIE
          You heard.

                    ACCOUNTANT
          And they're bad. You know, it's
          that, and it's the money that he's
          been lending to his father, that's
          creating a strain.

                    DEBBIE
          How much have we lent him?

                    ACCOUNTANT
          Eighty thousand.

                    DEBBIE
          Did you say "eight thousand" or
          "eighty thousand"?

                    ACCOUNTANT
          Eighty thousand, over the past
          couple of years. And then you
          missed the mortgage payment--

                    DEBBIE
          On the house?

                    ACCOUNTANT
          And you missed the rental on the
          office.

                    DEBBIE
          Does Pete know that?

                    ACCOUNTANT
          Oh, yeah. We're on the phone all
          the time. Look, I know you're going
          through a hard time, and I want you
          guys to know that we're here for
          you, okay? Anything you guys need,
          that's why we're here. We're here
          for times like this.

                    DEBBIE
          What are you going to do?

                    ACCOUNTANT
          There's not much I can do.

INT. RECORD LABEL - MORNING

Pete enters and walks into Ronnie's office. Ronnie is drawing
on a blackboard behind his desk.

                    PETE
          What are you doing?

                    RONNIE
          I'm drawing the album cover for Van
          Halen's *Diver Down*.

                    PETE
          If you spent a little bit more time
          focusing on Graham Parker instead
          of drawing album covers, I wouldn't
          be in this predicament.

                    RONNIE
          I'm focused on Graham Parker.

                    PETE
          You're supposed to help me with
          him!
                    (MORE)

                    PETE (CONT'D)
You're supposed to call the
companies, you're supposed to get
people to the show!

                    RONNIE
I've done everything I can, Pete.
You had me pushing around a corpse.
It was like being in fucking
Weekend at Graham's.

                    PETE
What should we do? I'm out of
ideas.

                    RONNIE
You fly in The Rumour. I can't sell
a reunion concert without the band.
It's ridiculous.

                    PETE
With what? I can't afford it.

                    RONNIE
You put this on yourself. You
wanted the responsibility, take it
on the chin, and stop acting like a
bitch.

                    PETE
What did you call me?

                    RONNIE
Chin.

Pete walks out of Ronnie's office and into the main office
space. Ronnie follows.

                    RONNIE (CONT'D)
Pete -- wait. I have an apartment,
I have health insurance, I have car
payments. I have responsibilities.

                    PETE
Don't talk to me about
responsibilities. I have a life. I
have a family. I can't afford to
sit in my apartment getting high,
jerking off, and then going to
Tommy's Chili Burgers at three in
the morning.

                    RONNIE
That's not even the order that
happens in!

                    PETE
          I have everything to lose here.
          Everything.

                    RONNIE
          Yes. Because you spent thousands of
          dollars on shit we don't need. You
          really need to spend thirty
          thousand dollars on a fucking neon
          sign, dude? Which is inside? It's
          not even outside. We know where we
          work.

                    PETE
          If you want to sign a band, you
          have to look like you're the real
          deal.

                    RONNIE
               (to Cat)
          Princess Labia, how much is it to
          fly The Rumour in?

                    CAT
          It's twelve thousand.

                    RONNIE
          Twelve thousand dollars!

                    PETE
          You know what? Fine. Fly in The
          Rumour. Put it on my AmEx.

INT. GYNECOLOGIST'S OFFICE - DAY

Debbie sits in Dr. Pelligrino's office.

                    DEBBIE
          No, you said it was impossible.

                    DR. PELLIGRINO
          I don't think I said it was
          impossible.

                    DEBBIE
          Yeah.

                    DR. PELLIGRINO
          I usually don't say impossible. I
          like to leave some wiggle room.

                    DEBBIE
          You said that my fibroid was like a
          giant boulder, like the one from
          the *Indiana Jones* movies blocking
          up my uterus.

                    DR. PELLIGRINO
          And I need to stop using that
          reference of *Indiana Jones*. I think
          that's not appropriate when talking
          about the reproductive system.

                    DEBBIE
          It's okay.

                    DR. PELLIGRINO
          Anyway, somehow the Eastern
          medicine has worked and the fibroid
          has dissipated.

                    DEBBIE
          That's great.

                    DR. PELLIGRINO
          Yes. Your fibroid shrunk, and
          somehow it allowed you to get
          pregnant.

                    DEBBIE
          What?

                    DR. PELLIGRINO
          You're going to have your third
          baby. Congratulations.

                    DEBBIE
          No.

                    DR. PELLIGRINO
          Yes.

Debbie does not react.

                    DR. PELLIGRINO (CONT'D)
          Would you like some water?

                    DEBBIE
          That's good news. Another baby, at
          forty.

                    DR. PELLIGRINO
          Debbie?

                    DEBBIE
          I am thrilled. And Pete is going to
          be so happy.

                    DR. PELLIGRINO
          So, you're okay?

                    DEBBIE
          What a relief. I can finally relax
          now, you know? I'm so happy, I
          really am. It's good.

                    DR. PELLIGRINO
          Great. Great.

INT. CAR - DAY

Debbie drives. We cannot tell what she is feeling. Then after
a few beats, a joyous smile appears across her face.

INT. RECORD LABEL - PETE'S OFFICE - DAY

Pete takes a framed item off of his wall.

EXT. LARRY'S HOUSE - DAY

Larry answers the door. Pete is there with a framed drawing
made by John Lennon.

                    PETE
          Hey, why are you in a bathrobe?
          It's the middle of the afternoon.

INT. LARRY'S HOUSE - CONTINUOUS

                    LARRY
          I took a late shower. Why are you
          busting my balls? Look, I'm sorry
          about the record. You're going
          through financial shit. This is
          what I live with. This is a
          horrible time in human history.
          What is that?

                    PETE
          Something that might help both of
          our situations.

Pete hands him the drawing.

                    PETE (CONT'D)
This is a drawing by John Lennon. I
got it ten years ago for five
thousand dollars. I don't know how
much it's worth now. Could be five,
could be twenty.

                    LARRY
I don't want this. I don't even
like it. I'm not going to hang it
up.

                    PETE
It's not for you to hang up. It's
for you to sell. That way I can
give it to you and you can make
some money, and Debbie doesn't know
that I'm giving you anything.

                    LARRY
Well, you're not giving me money.
You're giving me a project. I don't
know how to sell this. I'm not an
art dealer.

                    PETE
Just sell it online. Do some
research, make some calls. Or is
that too hard to do with your high
blood pressure?

                    LARRY
All right. Don't get snippy. Just
because you write a great song
doesn't mean you can draw.

                    PETE
It's incredible. John Lennon drew
it.

                    LARRY
I think it's a Ringo. Don't beat me
up if I get three hundred dollars
for it.

                    PETE
Don't take less than sixty-five
hundred for that. It's very
valuable. It's important to me. I
want you to sell it so I can help
you.

                    LARRY
Okay.

STILLS

"You guys are going to cherish each other one day."

"…just like, drift, into a coma, from which she never awakens."

"This is music that makes people happy."

"Well, I don't do that, but I will continue not to do that."

"Sadie. Sadie, Sadie!"

"We had sex the other night. You have to give me a little credit for that."

"I know how old you are. By counting the rings!"

"Don't jump on Daddy. Remember, Daddy has high blood what?"

"Make a fort? Outside? And do what in the fort?"

"I think this room has rodents."

"That's not even the order that happens in!"

"Why are you wearing a tank top? So you can show off your bald pits, you little hairless wonder."

This actually *was* the first performance in 30 years of Graham Parker and The Rumour.

"Let's fucking dance!"

"I don't want anyone to fight."

"He just touched my nipple!"

"That's what you look like. Like a bullshit bank commercial couple."

"Are you still upset about *Lost?*"

"Help me!"

"Now it starts here, but it used to start here."

"I'm ready to buff."

"Are there hunchbacks today?"

"You're making me embarrassed."

"You think our wives are looking at us right now?"

"We're not going to have an Asian baby. They're not Asian."

"I'm going to have some freaky ass nightmares."

The end.

                    PETE
          I'll see you at my party.

                    LARRY
          What should I bring? You want wine
          or something?

                    PETE
          No. Don't buy wine with my money
          and give it to me at my party.

                    LARRY
          That's mean.

                    PETE
          I love you. Bye.

                    LARRY
          All right. Bye... How do I call
          eBay?

INT. SCHOOL AUDITORIUM - DAY

Sadie and a bunch of other kids are building sets for a
school play. Sadie talks with a FRIEND.

Pete and Debbie are watching from afar, sitting next to each
other. Debbie tries to gently break the news.

                    DEBBIE
          She's so cute. She's so tall.

                    PETE
          I know. How did that happen?

                    DEBBIE
          Do you ever wish we had a bigger
          family?

                    PETE
          No, never for a second. Never.

                    DEBBIE
          Never?

                    PETE
          Never. I love what we have. One? A
          breeze. Two? Brutal. Three? Put a
          bullet in my head.

Debbie is totally deflated.

                          PETE (CONT'D)
          I think about that gray-haired
          pregnant lady from school and I
          just feel bad for her. And I feel
          bad for the kid. Can you imagine?
          All the other little kids, "Where's
          your mommy?" "Oh, she's the one
          sitting in that scooter eating a
          soft cracker." Kids don't want to
          have old parents. You know, it
          would also be nice for us to spend
          some time apart. Kind of rediscover
          who we are individually. It would
          be so great to not see you for like
          a chunk of time so that I could
          really just miss you. Remember when
          we used to miss each other?

EXT. SCHOOL - DAY

Debbie is walking through the campus upset. She sees a kid
and darts over to him.

                          DEBBIE
          Hey!

JOSEPH (13), the kid who insulted Sadie on her Facebook,
turns and sees Debbie.

                          JOSEPH
          Yo, sup?

                          DEBBIE
          I'm Sadie's mom.

                          JOSEPH
          Sadie...?

                          DEBBIE
          Sadie, the one you chat with on the
          internet?

                          JOSEPH
          Nah, man. That ain't me.

                          DEBBIE
          Well, it was you, I saw your
          picture. Did you make a "Hot" list
          and not put Sadie on the "Hot"
          list?

                          JOSEPH
          She was not on my list, no.

                    DEBBIE
          You know what I'm going to do? I'm
          going to make my own "Hot" list,
          and you know what? You're on the
          "Not Hot" list. How does that feel?

                    JOSEPH
          It doesn't bother me. I'm
          comfortable with the way I am.

She gets even quieter, scarier and more in his face.

                    DEBBIE
          Maybe you shouldn't be so
          comfortable with yourself. You know
          why? You look like a miniature Tom
          Petty. How's that feel? Huh? You
          think that haircut's cool? It's
          not. It looks like you put your
          Justin Bieber wig on backwards. You
          still comfortable with yourself?
          Why are you wearing a tank top?
          Huh? So you can show off your bald
          pits, you little hairless wonder?
          Cool tank top, man. So next time
          you think about writing something
          nasty on my daughter's Facebook
          page, just remember me. Remember
          me. I will come down here, and I
          will fuck you up.

Joseph looks upset.

                    JOSEPH
          Okay, I'm sorry.

                    DEBBIE
          Wait a minute. Hey. Are you crying?

                    JOSEPH
          Just let me go.

                    DEBBIE
          I'm sorry. I'm not in my right
          head.

                    JOSEPH
          I understand. My mom is going
          through menopause, too. It's a hard
          time.

                    DEBBIE
          What did you say?

              JOSEPH
      You're going through menopause?

              DEBBIE
      I'm not going through menopause!
      I'm not going to go through
      menopause for twenty years. I'm
      pregnant you little bitch. God damn
      it!

She storms off.

INT. MASTER BEDROOM - BATHROOM - NIGHT

Debbie pulls open the door, Pete is on the toilet playing on
his iPad.

              DEBBIE
      I'm going out to coffee with Desi
      to find out if she's stealing from
      us.

              PETE
      I've got the Graham Parker concert.
      Who's gonna watch the kids?

              DEBBIE
      I don't know. Figure it out.

Debbie exits. Pete flips her off after she's gone.

INT. BAR - NIGHT

Debbie and Desi are talking as they walk down the stairs into
a loud club.

              DEBBIE
      I just wanted to talk. Maybe we
      could go to a coffee house or
      something?

              DESI
      You want coffee? This place has
      coffee. They have all kinds of
      drinks.

INT. BAR - NIGHT

Debbie and Desi talk to a group of young men, PROFESSIONAL
HOCKEY PLAYERS.

                    DESI
          What sport do you guys play?

                    HOCKEY PLAYER
          We play hockey.

                    DESI
          Oh, I like hockey.

                    DEBBIE
          Who do you guys play for?

                    HOCKEY PLAYER
          We play for the Philadelphia
          Flyers.

                    DEBBIE
          You guys are all from Philadelphia?

                    HOCKEY PLAYER
          No, actually none of us are.

                    DESI
          Do you guys still have all of your
          teeth?

                    HOCKEY PLAYER #2
          Well, I've got all my teeth, except
          for these ones.

He takes a plate of his teeth out.

                    HOCKEY PLAYER #2 (CONT'D)
          Want to try them on?

Desi takes them and tries to put them in her mouth. Everyone
laughs.

                    DESI
          Do I look sexy?

Desi looks insane. She tries to kiss Debbie. Everyone is
laughing.

                    HOCKEY PLAYER #3
          They definitely look way better on
          her than they do on you.

She hands the teeth back to their owner. He pops them back in
and everyone cheers.

                    DEBBIE
          So, should we go to the quiet area?

                    HOCKEY PLAYERS
          No, no.

                    HOCKEY PLAYER #4
          Where are you going?

                    DEBBIE
          We kind of have to have a little
          business meeting tonight.

                    HOCKEY PLAYER
          Business meeting? You have to
          celebrate with us. We won tonight.

                    DESI
          I want to party with these winners,
          come on Deb.

                    HOCKEY PLAYER #4
          Come dance with us.

                    DEBBIE
               (thinks about it)
          Okay. Let's fucking dance! Yeah!

INT. NIGHTCLUB - NIGHT - CONTINUOUS

Pete on stage in a half-filled nightclub.

                    PETE
          Thank you so much for coming, this
          is so exciting! For the first time
          in over thirty years, Graham Parker
          and The Rumour.

Pete watches Graham Parker perform with his band. The song is
amazing. It is about issues Pete is going through, and he is
really connecting.

                    PETE (CONT'D)
               (to Ronnie)
          Where are his fans? Where are they?

                    RONNIE
          It's hard to watch a band when you
          know all of them remember D-Day.

                    PETE
          What's press turnout like?

                    RONNIE
          Are you serious? Nobody came.

                    PETE
          Nobody is here?

                    RONNIE
          Oh, the guy from Green Day is here.

BILLIE JOE ARMSTRONG sits nearby, watching the show.

                    PETE
          Yeah, Billie Joe, I emailed him.
          He's a fan.

                    RONNIE
          You've got to get a photo of the
          two of them.

                    PETE
          No, he says he doesn't want to do
          any press, he's just watching the
          show.

                    RONNIE
          Oh, how punk rock of him. "I don't
          like photographs."
               (to Billie Joe)
          Grow up, Green Day!

                    BILLIE JOE
          Shut up, Tom Selleck.

INT. NIGHTCLUB - NIGHT

Desi and Debbie dance with the hockey players to a Nikki
Minaj song. Debbie lets loose, she's having the time of her
life.

INT. NIGHTCLUB - MOMENTS LATER

Debbie is talking to a hockey player named JAY who is twenty-
four and cute.

                    JAY
          I wouldn't call them classically
          good dance moves, but you left it
          all out there. You're a blast to
          dance with.

                    DEBBIE
          Thank you.

                    JAY
We're having a little shindig at
the hotel after this, you should
come by and hang out.

                    DEBBIE
You want me to come to the hotel?

                    JAY
Yes. I want you to come by the
hotel with me.

                    DEBBIE
Well, what would we do there?

                    JAY
Maybe we can find somewhere quiet,
have fun, and see where it goes.
Like adults do sometimes.

                    DEBBIE
Like, sex?

                    JAY
I mean, if you want. If that's on
the docket. I'm not trying to force
that.

                    DEBBIE
So you would do sex with me?

                    JAY
Do sex? What are you, Borat?

                    DEBBIE
Are you hitting on me?

                    JAY
Yes. I'm hitting on you. You're hot
and cool and nice and you have
beautiful eyes.

                    DEBBIE
I'm sorry. I'm married, I have two
kids, and I'm pregnant.

                    JAY
That is what we call the "hat
trick." Wow.

                    DEBBIE
I'm sorry I didn't tell you. I'm
just really enjoying you being so
nice to me.

                    JAY
          I hope this doesn't come off as
          super cheesy, but I think you're a
          very rare find.

                    DEBBIE
          Thank you.

                    JAY
          And I would totally do sex with
          you.

They laugh.

INT. NIGHTCLUB - LATER

Graham is packing up to go. Pete approaches him.

                    PETE
               (to the band)
          That was spectacular guys, really
          well done.
               (to Graham)
          Hey, Graham.

                    GRAHAM
          Pete! How are you, man?

                    PETE
          Well, the first numbers came in.

                    GRAHAM
          Happy? How's it looking?

                    PETE
          About half of your last record.

                    GRAHAM
          Ah, so you were expecting it to
          sell. They never sell anymore. They
          used to sell. But now they don't.
          I'm not a sexy sixteen-year-old
          girl.

                    PETE
          But I wanted to sell it. It's such
          a good record. I feel like I let
          you down.

                    GRAHAM
          No, I'm going to be fine. My
          overheads are so low. I just got a
          song in *Glee*.
               (MORE)

                    GRAHAM (CONT'D)
          Guy in the wheelchair is going to
          sing it to the Asian girl, I
          believe. I don't know, I've never
          seen the show, but that's what I'm
          told. Secret is, make sure you have
          a small nut. That's the key to
          life.

                    PETE
          Graham, I don't have small nuts,
          all right? I have big nuts. And I
          need to provide for them.

Billie Joe comes over to congratulate Graham.

                    BILLIE JOE
          Graham, hey, what's up?

                    GRAHAM
          Billie!

                    BILLIE JOE
          How you doing, man? Great show. I'm
          inspired. I want to write a song
          right now.

                    GRAHAM
          Inspired, huh? That inspires me.

                    BILLIE JOE
          Let's go get a drink.

                    GRAHAM
          Let's get a drink.

                    BILLIE JOE
              (to Pete)
          You coming?

                    PETE
          No. I'm fine. You guys go.
          Congratulations on *Glee*.

They walk away.

                    BILLIE JOE
          You got a song on *Glee*? That's
          killer, man. That's so much money,
          that's good for all of us.

INT. CAR - NIGHT

Pete sits in the car crying.

INT. CAR - NIGHT

Debbie is dropping Desi off at her apartment.

                    DEBBIE
          Why did you put that guy's teeth in
          your mouth? That's so gross. He was
          dirty.

                    DESI
          No, he was wearing a tie.

                    DEBBIE
          That's true.

                    DESI
          When I kissed him, I felt his
          little tiny teeth nubs with my
          tongue.

                    DEBBIE
          You did?

                    DESI
          It was like kissing a baby. French
          kissing a baby.

                    DEBBIE
          Can I ask you something stupid? Do
          you know why we're missing money at
          the store?

                    DESI
          Are you guys missing money?

                    DEBBIE
          Like twelve thousand dollars.

                    DESI
          Wait. Do you think I took it?

                    DEBBIE
          Well, no. I did, but now I don't.

                    DESI
          It's not me.

                    DEBBIE
          Then, why do you live in such a
          nice apartment and have such a
          fancy car?

                         DESI
          Yes, you're right. Look. I... am an
          escort. I get paid to go out on
          dates.

Debbie looks shocked.

                         DESI (CONT'D)
          But only three to five times a
          year. Ten times max. But it's not
          technically "prostitution" because
          I don't have to sleep with them.

                         DEBBIE
          Well, that's good.

                         DESI
          But I always do. That's why I only
          do it four to eight times a year,
          fifteen times max.

                         DEBBIE
          Huh.

                         DESI
          One year I did it twenty.

                         DEBBIE
          As long as you think it's safe.

                         DESI
          It's safe. I only do it ten to
          thirty times a year.

                         DEBBIE
          So, who do you think is stealing
          money?

                         DESI
          It's Jodi.

                         DEBBIE
          No.

                         DESI
          Yeah. She's a pilled-out whore.

                         DEBBIE
          Since you told me, I want to tell
          you something.

                         DESI
          You're pregnant.

                    DEBBIE
          How did you know?

Desi nods.

                    DEBBIE (CONT'D)
          Wow. Maybe you should tell Pete.

                    DESI
          You didn't tell Pete yet? Why not?

                    DEBBIE
          I don't know. I just want him to
          want me. I don't want him to want
          me because I'm pregnant.

                    DESI
          Go home and suck his dick and tell
          him then and he will love it.

                    DEBBIE
          You think?

                    DESI
          He'll be so excited. Or even better
          yet, you should tell him while
          you're sucking his dick.
               (mimes a blow job)
          "I'm pregnant."

INT. BEDROOM - NEXT MORNING

Pete on his iPad laying in bed. Debbie comes in to talk.

                    DEBBIE
          What are you doing?

                    PETE
          I'm returning some emails.

                    DEBBIE
          What time do you have to go to
          work?

                    PETE
          Like ten minutes ago.

                    DEBBIE
          Want to be late?

Debbie's shirt is unbuttoned and she is topless.

                         PETE
                    (not looking up)
          No, I can't be late. Not today.

Pause.

                         DEBBIE
          Do you see me? Standing here in
          front of you? Half-naked?

                         PETE
          Yeah.

                         DEBBIE
          And does that make you feel
          anything?

                         PETE
          Come on. Are you trying to start a
          fight?

                         DEBBIE
          No, I'm not trying to start a fight
          with you. I'm trying to fuck you!

                         PETE
          Oh god, you know what? Today of all
          days you need to give me a break,
          all right?

                         DEBBIE
          Whatever.

She exits into the bathroom. There's silence.

                         PETE
          I didn't realize it was
          intentional! I didn't say anything
          because I didn't want you to be
          embarrassed. I thought I was being
          gallant.

No response.

                         PETE (CONT'D)
          All right, fine, I'm an asshole.

Debbie returns, dressed.

                         DEBBIE
          You know what your problem is?
          You're never in the moment, you're
          never present. You're never in your
          body.

> PETE
> That's not true. I am in the
> moment. You know how I know? I want
> to get the fuck out of the moment.
> I swear, I can't win with you.

Pete walks out of the room. Debbie follows.

> DEBBIE
> You can't just walk away.

INT. PETE'S OFFICE - CONTINUOUS

> DEBBIE
> How's the record company going,
> Pete?

> PETE
> What? Not great. I'm still waiting
> for numbers to come in.

> DEBBIE
> What have you heard?

> PETE
> A couple numbers have trickled in.
> It's lower than we expected.

> DEBBIE
> Then why are you giving Larry
> money?

> PETE
> What?

> DEBBIE
> I know everything. I talked to the
> accountant.

> PETE
> All right, you know what? I don't
> want to get into some nasty fight.
> So can we please talk to each other
> like the therapist told us to talk
> to each other?

> DEBBIE
> Fine. It makes me feel sad when you
> are dishonest.

> PETE
> I understand it makes you feel bad
> when I am dishonest with you.
> (MORE)

                    PETE (CONT'D)
It hurts my feelings when you treat
me with contempt and corner me and
try and trick me into lying.

                    DEBBIE
Okay. It makes me sad when it's so
easy to trick you into lying
because you're such a lying
shitbag.

                    PETE
You can't do that. The therapist
said you're not allowed to judge
me.

                    DEBBIE
That's not a judgment. That's just
a fact.

                    PETE
Fair enough. Sometimes I withhold
truth, that is true. But it's only
because I'm scared to death of your
crazy-assed illogical
overreactions.

                    DEBBIE
Well, it hurts me inside and
triggers me that you're such a
dishonest shit that you're lending
your father money without telling
me, while your record company is
going bankrupt and we're on the
verge of losing our fucking house!

INT. CHARLOTTE'S ROOM - CONTINUOUS

Charlotte plays piano in her room alone. Through the wall,
she can hear Debbie and Pete fighting.

INT. BEDROOM - CONTINUOUS

                    DEBBIE
What else are you lying about?

                    PETE
I've taken Viagra for two years. I
ate six muffins downstairs a while
ago and my cholesterol level is
305. My heart could explode at any
second. These might be my very last
words.
                    (MORE)

                    PETE (CONT'D)
And I gave Charlotte antibiotics
when you weren't looking. That's
why her ear got better. So, go fuck
your witch doctor.

                    DEBBIE
What are we even doing? This is not
making me happy. You're not happy.
You don't like me. I can feel that.
I'm not blind. Jesus. We're like
business associates. We're like
brother and sister. There's no
passion there.

                    PETE
We're not like brother and sister.
You know what we're like? We're
like Simon and Garfunkel, and
somehow you turned me into
Garfunkel.

                    DEBBIE
I don't even know what that means.

                    PETE
Art Garfunkel.

                    DEBBIE
What's wrong with Art Garfunkel? He
has a beautiful voice.

                    PETE
He's got an amazing voice. He could
put a harmony to anything, but what
I'm saying is that you turned me
into him.

                    DEBBIE
What the hell are you talking
about?

                    PETE
Simon controls him.

                    DEBBIE
That's because Simon writes the
fucking songs! He's the better one.

                    PETE
You know what? I see the way you
look at our kids. You have so much
love and compassion for them. You
never look at me like that. Ever.

                    DEBBIE
          Would we even still be together if
          I didn't get pregnant fourteen
          years ago?

                    PETE
          I'm not going to go down that road.

                    DEBBIE
          Would we?

Pete doesn't say anything.

                    DEBBIE (CONT'D)
          Okay.

Debbie starts walking away.

                    DEBBIE (CONT'D)
          You know what? I don't even want to
          have a party here. You need to
          cancel it.

                    PETE
          No, I'm not. I already paid for the
          catering, I put down deposits, and
          I'm not going to call everybody
          back in two days when you change
          your mind.

INT. BEDROOM - NIGHT

They all are laying in bed watching *Spongebob Squarepants*. It
is tense. Charlotte is licking her fingers.

                    SADIE
          Can you please stop licking your
          fingers?

Charlotte does it more.

                    SADIE (CONT'D)
          Do you know how many germs are on
          your hands? And you're putting them
          into your mouth. It's gross. Stop.

Charlotte pokes Sadie with her wet fingers.

                    SADIE (CONT'D)
          I'm going to kill you!

                         PETE
              Hey! Sadie, enough! She isn't
              hurting anyone. If you want to say
              something, keep your mouth shut.

                         DEBBIE
              You have never been nice to her and
              now she's getting aggressive with
              you. I told you this would happen.

Sadie leaves and slams her door.

                         CHARLOTTE
              I'm sick of everybody fighting.

Charlotte leaves.

INT. CHARLOTTE'S ROOM - NIGHT - LATER

Charlotte writes a note at her desk.

INT. HALLWAY/SADIE'S ROOM - NIGHT

Charlotte walks by Sadie's room. She puts the note up on the
door. It reads, "I'm sorry you think I'm gross. You are
right. Love, Charlotte."

INT. HOME OFFICE - NIGHT

Pete sits alone, listening to music.

INT. LIVING ROOM - NIGHT

Sadie sits alone watching *Lost* on an iPad.

INT. CHARLOTTE'S ROOM - NIGHT - LATER

Debbie rests next to Charlotte in bed.

                         DEBBIE
              What do you think you're going to
              be like when you grow up?

                         CHARLOTTE
              I don't know.

                         DEBBIE
              Do you think you want kids?

                    CHARLOTTE
          Just one.

                    DEBBIE
          Just one? Why?

                    CHARLOTTE
          Because if I have two then the one
          will fight with the other one.

                    DEBBIE
          Does it make you sad when you
          fight?

                    CHARLOTTE
          I don't want anyone to fight.

                    DEBBIE
          I love you.

INT. FAMILY ROOM - MORNING

Pete is sleeping on the couch.

INT. KITCHEN - MORNING

Pete sits at the counter. Debbie and the kids are at the
breakfast table.

                    CHARLOTTE
          Why isn't anybody talking? Why is
          it so quiet?

                    PETE
          It's the sounds of silence.

INT. CAR - DAY

Pete is driving Sadie and Charlotte to school. On the stereo
is "Paradise by the Dashboard Light" by Meatloaf. Pete is
eating an egg sandwich and manically singing along.

                    PETE
              (singing)
          I don't think that I can really
          survive... I'm praying for the end
          of time, it's all that I can do.
          Praying for the end of time, so I
          can end my time with you.

                    SADIE
Stop, Dad.

                    PETE
It was long ago and it was far
away, it was so much better than it
is today.

                    CHARLOTTE
How many of those are you going to
eat?

                    PETE
As many as I want.

                    CHARLOTTE
I'm going to tell Mom on you.

                    PETE
Try it. See what you get for
Christmas. Nothing. Snitches wind
up in ditches. Remember that.

EXT. SCHOOL - DAY

Pete walks Charlotte in. He gives her a kiss then walks back
towards his car. On the way he bumps into Joseph and his mom,
CATHERINE.

                    CATHERINE
        Peter!

                    PETE
        Hey.

                    CATHERINE
Catherine. I'm Joseph's mother.

                    PETE
        (pleasantly lying)
Oh, right. No, I know. Hi,
Catherine.

                    CATHERINE
Our kids have gone to school
together for eight years.

                    PETE
Sorry.
        (to Joseph)
Hello, Joseph.
        (to Catherine)
                    (MORE)

                    PETE (CONT'D)
I hear our kids have been chatting
online.

                    CATHERINE
Yeah? I heard that your wife has
been screaming at my son and I
don't appreciate it.

                    PETE
Excuse me?

                    CATHERINE
She screamed at my son.
     (to Joseph)
Right? She threatened you?
     (to Pete)
She cursed at him. He's thirteen
years old for god's sake. What the
hell is the matter with her? You
better check her meds and get them
right.

Pete thinks for a moment, not sure how to handle this.

                    PETE
Okay, why don't you back the fuck
off, because that's my lovely,
sweet wife you're talking about.

                    CATHERINE
Oh, I need to back off?

                    PETE
Yeah, you need to back off because
your kid is an animal. Why don't
you put him on a leash?

                    CATHERINE
     (to Joseph)
Turn around!

                    PETE
If he insults my daughter again,
I'm going to hit him with my car.
Got it? In fact, if you insult my
wife again, you know what I'm going
to do? I'm going to show up at your
house when you're sleeping, and
I'll take your iPad and your iPod
or your iMac and I'll shove them up
your fucking iCunt. I've got
nothing to lose. Your kid is the
problem. My kid is a fucking angel.
I don't have time for this shit.
                    (MORE)

                    PETE (CONT'D)
So I'm keeping it together. But if
I wasn't at school right now...

He pokes her shoulder.

                    CATHERINE
Don't touch me.

                    PETE
I didn't touch you.

                    CATHERINE
You touched my upper breast!

                    PETE
I didn't. I got right below your
shoulder.

                    CATHERINE
You got right here.
     (to Joseph)
He hit my nipple!

                    JOSEPH
You what?

                    PETE
You're insane.

                    CATHERINE
Why would you do that?

                    JOSEPH
Did you just touch my mom's nipple?

                    CATHERINE
He just touched my nipple! Why
would you do that?

                    PETE
I poked you on the shoulder.

                    CATHERINE
I have very high nipples.

                    PETE
I touched your shirt.

                    CATHERINE
What do you think is under my
shirt? My breasts are under my
shirt.
     (to Joseph)
He just touched my breast.

                    PETE
          Your shoulder, your shoulder.

                    CATHERINE
          That's a funny place to put a
          shoulder. My boob!

                    PETE
          Hello! There are children around.

                    CATHERINE
          This isn't over. You're going to be
          sorry.
               (to Joseph)
          Let's go!

INT. COFFEE BEAN AND TEA LEAF - DAY

Debbie is talking to Jodi, who is crying.

                    JODI
          Why the fuck would you believe
          Desi?

                    DEBBIE
          You just admitted it.

                    JODI
          Did I?

                    DEBBIE
          You stole twelve thousand dollars
          from me, Jodi, and I need you to
          pay me back.

                    JODI
          Can you at least give me a
          referral?

                    DEBBIE
          You babysat my kids while you were
          on Oxycontin.

                    JODI
          Oxycotton.

                    DEBBIE
          Oxyconton?

                    JODI
          Oxykitten.

                    DEBBIE
What's oxykitten?

                    JODI
Meow.

                    DEBBIE
Jodi. You put me in danger. Me and
my family.

                    JODI
It was a cry for help. Help.
     (getting weirder)
Help. Why don't you help me? Just
help. Help. Why don't you help me?

                    DEBBIE
Are you high right now?

                    JODI
     (weirder)
Help me.

Debbie's phone buzzes.

                    JODI (CONT'D)
Is that about me? Is that the cops?
Is this a set-up?

                    DEBBIE
I need to go.

                    JODI
Okay, see you later.
     (creepily)
Fuck you, Debbie. Fuck. You.

INT. VICE PRINCIPAL'S OFFICE - DAY

Pete and Debbie are sitting across from VICE PRINCIPAL
LAVIANI. In another seat is Joseph's mother, Catherine.

                    MS. LAVIANI
Joseph was very upset when I spoke
to him about this, so I thought it
was important that we join together
and work this through.

                    PETE
Absolutely.

                    CATHERINE
          We're going to work through it, but
          Debbie told my son that he looked
          like Tom Petty, in a negative way--

                    PETE
          Who's Tom Petty?

                    CATHERINE
          You know who Tom Petty is. And she
          said that if she had to come back,
          that she was going to "F up his
          pussy ass." Which is what she said.

                    DEBBIE
          Are you serious? I didn't. I would
          never. To a child? Your son has
          been defiling my daughter's
          Facebook page now for months.

                    CATHERINE
          These people are liars. He said
          that my son was an animal and that
          if I didn't keep him on a leash
          that he would hit him with his car.

                    MS. LAVIANI
          Did you say that?

                    PETE
          That's ridiculous. Who talks like
          that?

                    CATHERINE
          You do.

Debbie tries to hide a smile.

                    DEBBIE
          He didn't say that.

                    CATHERINE
          He said it. To me.

                    PETE
          What I said was that we need to
          keep an extra eye on our kids
          because with all the technological
          advances, they need to learn to use
          them responsibly.

                    CATHERINE
          No. He called me an "iCunt."

                    PETE
A what?

                    MS. LAVIANI
Language, Catherine!

                    CATHERINE
How am I going to relay what these
two nutballs said to me unless I
say it.

                    MS. LAVIANI
Can you please not talk like that,
Catherine? *Music Man* is rehearsing
next door.

                    CATHERINE
Sorry, fucking *Music Man*. Maybe if
I looked more like this fake
bullshit couple, looks like they're
in a bank commercial. That's what
you look like. Like a bullshit bank
commercial couple.

                    MS. LAVIANI
None of this talk is productive.

                    CATHERINE
I'd like to rear up and jackknife
my legs and kick you both in the
jaw with my foot bone.

                    DEBBIE
You're just really scaring me.

                    CATHERINE
This is what happens when you
corner a rat. You corner me, I will
chew through you.

                    MS. LAVIANI
Catherine, you're better than this.

                    CATHERINE
Fuck you, Jill. You're a horrible
woman. This is why everybody hates
you. This kind of shit.
Ineffective. Bullshit hair. And I'm
glad your husband died. Because
you're a fucking asshole. He
probably killed himself.

                    MS. LAVIANI
          Okay, Catherine. I think we know
          what's happening now.

                    DEBBIE
          Now you know what we're dealing
          with.

EXT. PARKING LOT - DAY

Pete and Debbie leave the school together, surpressing
smiles. They get in separate cars and drive off.

INT. KITCHEN - NIGHT

Debbie is making dinner. Pete and Charlotte sit at the table.

                    CHARLOTTE
          I'm not going to eat that chicken.

                    DEBBIE
          Why not?

                    CHARLOTTE
          Because I feel like I'm going to be
          a vegetarian.

                    DEBBIE
          Can you become a vegetarian
          tomorrow?

                    CHARLOTTE
          No.

Sadie storms in.

                    SADIE
          You guys have been reading my
          texts?

                    PETE
          No, we haven't.

                    DEBBIE
          Yes, we have. We're supposed to
          keep an eye on you.

                    PETE
          How did you find out?

                    SADIE
Joseph told me that you flipped out
on him and his mom and that you
guys are nuts, and I agree.

                    PETE
Don't be disrespectful.

                    SADIE
You're the ones who are
disrespectful. Reading my texts is
like reading my diary.

                    DEBBIE
You were really sweet on your
iChat. We were really proud of you.

                    PETE
Yeah, we were going to give you
your computer and phone back.

                    SADIE
Fuck you!

                    PETE
Okay, there's the first official
"Fuck you."

                    DEBBIE
That is not how we talk to each
other in this house.

                    SADIE
You guys talk to each other like
that all the time! And to Joseph
and his mom. You made Joseph cry.

                    CHARLOTTE
Joseph has a crush on you. You like
a boy who cries.

                    SADIE
Shut up, Charlotte. You guys so
desperately want me to be perfect
and to make no mistakes. Well, you
two are fucking insane.

                    DEBBIE
Okay.

                    SADIE
          All you do is fight. Or you don't
          fight, which is even worse because
          it looks like you hate each other
          for weeks. You obsess over every
          little thing I do, and you don't
          trust in me or believe in me. Well,
          I'm fucking sick of it! Yeah, I
          said "fuck." Fuck fuck fuck. Ground
          me forever I don't care. I don't
          care about anything.
               (crying hard)
          I hate everything, everyone's going
          crazy, I don't care if I have no
          friends.

                    DEBBIE
          Are you still upset about *Lost*?

                    SADIE
          Of course I'm upset about *Lost*! You
          guys took away my shit before I
          could watch the last two episodes!
          I don't know what the fuck happens!

She walks off.

                    DEBBIE
          She's becoming just like us.

                    CHARLOTTE
          I hope I never get my period if
          this is what happens.

INT. SADIE'S ROOM - NIGHT

Sadie does her homework on her bed. Charlotte brings in
Sadie's electronics and puts them down in a pile beside her.

                    SADIE
          Where did you find these?

                    CHARLOTTE
          I stole them.

Charlotte walks away and starts to slide the door closed
behind her.

                    SADIE
          Thank you.

                    CHARLOTTE
          No big deal.

INT. LIVING ROOM - NIGHT

Debbie is sitting on the couch. Pete paces around the room.

                    PETE
          Our kids are crazy. And it's our
          fault.

                    DEBBIE
          Do you think there's anything we
          can do to turn it around?

                    PETE
          Sadie's thirteen. She might be a
          lost cause.

                    DEBBIE
          Where did she learn that kind of
          language? We don't talk like that.

                    PETE
          I have no fucking idea... Do you
          think Sadie is this crazy because
          of us? Or is it hormones and *Lost*.

                    DEBBIE
          J.J. Abrams. He's ruining our
          daughter. That fucking geek.

                    PETE
          I feel bad for us.

                    DEBBIE
          All of a sudden we're like a magnet
          for negativity. Why do people keep
          attacking us? What did we do? We're
          just doing our best.

                    PETE
          Should we talk about our fight?

                    DEBBIE
          I think we're under enough
          pressure. Let's just let it go this
          time.

                    PETE
          Yeah.

                    DEBBIE
          We can give each other a break.

                    PETE
Great. Thank you. And I'm sorry
about my dad. You're right. I'm
sorry that he's just an endless
mooch.
     (beat)
The truth is, this isn't about us.
It's about our parents.

                    DEBBIE
We're not even mad at each other.
We're mad at them.

                    PETE
Exactly.

                    DEBBIE
Let's just take away our parents'
power by loving them.

                    PETE
Can we do that?

                    DEBBIE
Yes.

                    PETE
Thank god.

                    DEBBIE
I kind of feel better already, do
you?

                    PETE
I do.

                    DEBBIE
I love you.

                    PETE
I love you too.

                    DEBBIE
It's not us, it's them.

                    PETE
Totally.

They hug.

INT. SADIE'S ROOM - MORNING

The shades are closed and the room is dark. Sadie watches the end of the last episode of *Lost* on a laptop. Pete enters.

> PETE
> What are you doing? We need to get ready for the party.

> SADIE
> (devastated)
> I just finished the last episode of *Lost*.

> PETE
> We don't have time for this right now. We have a lot of people coming over--

> SADIE
> (losing it)
> They're all dead.

> PETE
> What?

> SADIE
> Jack, Kate, Sawyer...

> PETE
> I don't care about the show right now-

> SADIE
> Jin, Sun...

> PETE
> Okay? I need you to just get in the shower. Get dressed. Let's just put it on hold.

> SADIE
> Walt, Juliet. All those people.

> PETE
> Don't think about *Lost* today. Tomorrow: *Lost*. All day. I can't wait to hear about it. Jack? No way. Really? Right now, shower.

> SADIE
> I don't make fun of your stupid *Mad Men*.

                    PETE
          First of all, I don't get worked up
          over *Mad Men*.

                    SADIE
          That's because *Mad Men* sucks.

                    PETE
          What Don Draper has gone through
          beats whatever Jack is running from
          on some island.

                    SADIE
          A bunch of people smoking in an
          office, it's stupid.

                    PETE
          You're getting me off topic. Please
          get dressed.

EXT. HOUSE - DAY

Debbie is speaking with Barb as they set up the kitchen for a
barbecue for Pete's fortieth birthday.

                    DEBBIE
          I am so glad you're here. I need a
          buffer in case it gets weird.

                    BARB
          Well, I'm ready to buff.

                    DEBBIE
          Here, grab these napkins.

INT./EXT. HOUSE - DAY

Desi jumps in the pool in a small bikini. She is playing in
the water with the kids.

ANGLE ON BARRY AND PETE

                    BARRY
          So that's the girl who works for
          you.

                    PETE
          Yeah, that's her.

                    BARRY
          Seems nice. My wife would never let
          me have a hot employee like that.
                    (MORE)

                         BARRY (CONT'D)
              Everyone that works for us looks
              like they've been in some kind of
              horrible accident.

Angle on Barb and Debbie.

                         BARB
              You're comfortable with that around
              your husband?

                         DEBBIE
              Pete wouldn't know what to do with
              that.

Angle on Barry and Pete.

                         BARRY
              You think our wives are looking at
              us right now?

                         PETE
              Oh, definitely.

Angle on Barb and Debbie.

                         DEBBIE
              They look like pedophiles.

Barry and Pete turn toward their wives, smile and wave.

INT. KITCHEN - LATER

Pete greets guests, including Graham and Grandma Molly.

EXT. BACKYARD - LATER

Pete and Ronnie are talking in the backyard.

                         DEBBIE (O.C.)
              Hey, Pete!

Debbie walks over with Jason.

                         DEBBIE (CONT'D)
              Jason's here.

                         JASON
              Peter, hi.

                         PETE
              Hey, how's it going?

                    JASON
          Great, you look well. How do you
          like what I've been doing to your
          girl? How do you like Debbie's
          after body?

                    RONNIE
          It's nice.

                    JASON
          Come on, show 'em. Look at this.
               (points to her ass)
          It's beautiful. Look at that after-
          ass. Now it starts here, but it
          used to start here. And I brought
          it up. You're welcome.

                    RONNIE
          Are you a trainer?

                    JASON
          Yes, well, but not just physical.
          Spiritual. I'm sort of a guide.

                    PETE
          You guys should talk. I think
          you'll get along. Come here, honey,
          I have to tell you something.

They leave Ronnie and Jason alone. The guys spot Desi
swimming in the pool.

                    JASON
          Who's that in the pool?

                    RONNIE
          Mine.

INT./EXT. FRONT DOOR - DAY

Debbie and Pete open the front door. Standing there is
Oliver. He gives a nervous smile.

Debbie looks at him and tries to be nice, but we feel her
effort.

                    DEBBIE
          Hello.

                    OLIVER
          Hello, Debbie.

She opens the door wider. They do not hug.

                         DEBBIE
              Remember my husband, Pete?

                         OLIVER
              Oh, yes. I didn't recognize you
              with the long hair.

                         PETE
                    (people pleasing)
              I've been growing it.

                         OLIVER
              Happy birthday.

He hands him a bottle.

                         PETE
              Thank you so much.

                         OLIVER
              Very old scotch.

                         PETE
              Oh, wow. You know, I hope it hasn't
              expired.

                         OLIVER
              No, scotch doesn't expire. It
              improves with age.

                         PETE
              No, I know. Thank you so much.

EXT. BACKYARD - DAY

The party is in full swing. Pete, Debbie, Oliver, Barry and
Barb are getting food from the buffet. Barb and Barry are
trying to help keep the conversation going.

                         BARRY
              What do you do in Chino, Oliver?

                         OLIVER
              I am a surgeon.

                         BARB
              Wow, what kind?

                         OLIVER
              Mainly of the spine. My specialty
              is scoliosis surgery.

> BARRY
> My mom used to talk to me like I
> had scoliosis because I'm a little
> hunchy, but that's a different
> thing.

> OLIVER
> Well, you definitely don't look
> right.

Larry arrives, with Claire and the triplets. Claire is
holding two of them, while Larry carries one.

The triplets now have very different HAIRCUTS so he can tell
them apart. One has a faux hawk, one has bangs, and one has a
buzz cut.

> LARRY
> Hello everyone! I'm sorry we're
> late. I was in the lab cloning
> myself. We're going to have another
> seven more tomorrow... Look, we cut
> their hair different so we can
> finally tell who they are.

Larry lifts one of the triplets up and down by the arms,
simulating an elevator.

> LARRY (CONT'D)
> You like the new haircut, Travis?

> TRIPLET #1
> I'm Jack, damn it.

> LARRY
> Of course you are.

Larry puts Jack down and he runs off.

> DEBBIE
> Larry, this is my father.

> LARRY
> Really? How are you?

> OLIVER
> Oliver.

> LARRY
> Oliver. "Can I have some more?
> Please, Oliver, I need a little
> morsel." I love that movie. You
> must get that all the time.

                    OLIVER
          Not really.

                    CLAIRE
          I'm Claire, Larry's wife. Very good
          to see you, but excuse me, I'm
          going to go get the kids.

Claire runs off.

                    LARRY
          We won't see her now for the whole
          day. I'd help honey, but I've got
          the blood pressure, and I don't
          want to.

                    PETE
          Dad, you want a drink?

                    LARRY
          Yeah, a little white wine.

                    PETE
          White wine? Okay, heavy stuff.

                    LARRY
          So, who knew that Debbie had a dad!
          Where have you been for fifteen
          years? Never seen you at Hanukkah,
          Christmas, Ramadan, nothing. How do
          you get out of all that stuff? Do
          you have a wife?

                    OLIVER
          My wife is at home.

                    DEBBIE
          Why didn't she come?

                    OLIVER
          Construction. They're sanding our
          deck.

                    LARRY
          You let the woman sand the deck?

                    OLIVER
          She supervises it, yes.

Sadie, Charlotte and Desi walk over.

                    DEBBIE
          Hey guys.

                    LARRY
          Look how big the kids are. Sadie!

He gives Desi a hug.

                    DESI
          Hi, Larry.

                    LARRY
               (to Sadie)
          Hi, Sadie.

                    SADIE
          Mom. Who is Oliver?

                    DEBBIE
          What do you mean?

                    CHARLOTTE
          Is he your dad?

                    DEBBIE
          He is my biological father.

                    CHARLOTTE
          What does that mean?

                    DEBBIE
          He and my mom had a baby and that
          was me.

                    SADIE
          Oh, so you're our grandpa.

                    OLIVER
          Why don't you ask your mother?

                    DEBBIE
          Yes, well, that would make him your
          grandpa. Do you want him to be?

                    CHARLOTTE
          Yes. Then we get another grandpa.
          Come on!

Oliver gets up. Charlotte, Sadie and Desi run off. Oliver
follows.

                    LARRY
          That was deeply uncomfortable.
          Thank god the pretty girl was here
          to divert our attention.

EXT. POOL - DAY

Desi is gracefully swimming under water. She looks gorgeous.
She sees Jason and Ronnie under water, but they look
grotesque, red-faced and awkward. They both reach for each
other and come to the surface.

                    JASON
          Oh, hi. I did not see you there.

                    RONNIE
          I saw you there.

                    DESI
          Did you guys come together? Are you
          a couple?

                    RONNIE / JASON
          No, we didn't come together.
          Absolutely not.

                    DESI
          Sorry, the mustache is a little--

                    JASON
          That's fair.

                    DESI
          I just assumed.

                    RONNIE
          This is a straight man mustache.

                    DESI
          What is the different between a gay
          man's mustache and a straight man's
          mustache?

Pause.

                    JASON
          The smell.

                    DESI
          Excuse me.

Desi swims away.

EXT. BACKYARD - LATER

Larry is talking to Oliver.

                    LARRY
So, spinal surgery just seems to me
to be at the top of the surgery
chain.

                    OLIVER
Well, we're not cardio, we're not
neuro, but I like to think we're an
important part of the spectrum.

                    LARRY
Do you operate every single day?

                    OLIVER
Most days.

                    LARRY
Multiple times a day?

                    OLIVER
Three, four times.

                    LARRY
So what's the price range? Like if
I wanted--

                    OLIVER
Oh, I'd rather not say.

                    LARRY
It's so big you're embarrassed to
say.

                    OLIVER
I wouldn't say embarrassed.

                    LARRY
Are there hunchbacks today?

                    OLIVER
Of course.

                    LARRY
I've never seen one.

                    OLIVER
Well, that's because there are
spinal surgeons.

                    LARRY
That's because of you. Each time I
don't see a hunchback, you're
getting that much richer.

Oliver smiles, amused.

> LARRY (CONT'D)
> You like The Beatles, don't you?

> OLIVER
> Who doesn't like The Beatles?

> LARRY
> Nobody.

EXT. POOLSIDE - DAY

Jason and Ronnie are talking to Desi.

> DESI
> So what's your sun sign?

> RONNIE
> Libra.

> JASON
> Oh, boy.

> DESI
> That's not good.

> JASON
> No, sir.

> DESI
> Not for me, that's not good.
> Sexually we are completely
> incompatible.

> RONNIE
> That's not true.

> JASON
> That's such a shame. That's as bad
> as it gets.

> DESI
> What's yours?

> JASON
> I'm a Cancer.

> DESI
> Really?

> JASON
> Is that good?

                    RONNIE
          What does it mean?

                    DESI
          That's really strange. Well, Taurus
          and Cancers are sort of soul mates
          of the Zodiac. We're like perfectly
          compatible. I balance what you
          lack, and you make up for what I
          lack. And a quiet Cancer almost
          always has a huge penis.

                    JASON
               (quietly)
          You're making me embarrassed.

EXT. BACKYARD - LATER

Debbie, Pete, Larry, Oliver, Barb and Barry are eating.

                    DEBBIE
          I wanted to make a toast. Thank you
          guys so much for coming... Pete's
          turning forty.

                    PETE
          Weird.

                    DEBBIE
          And we're ready to start this new
          phase of our lives with open
          hearts. Ready to just choose joy
          and forgive everybody, so thank you
          all for coming.

                    LARRY
          Wait. Forgive who?

                    PETE
          I think she just meant generally.
          You know? Put the past behind us.

                    DEBBIE
          And live without resentments.

                    LARRY
          But specifically who are you
          forgiving? I like to know the
          details before I toast.

                    DEBBIE
          Well, you and my dad and others.

                    LARRY
          I see. I know you have some issues
          with me, but I'm curious, what's he
          in for? Before today nobody even
          knew he existed.

                    DEBBIE
          My parents divorced when I was
          really young and we don't spend
          that much time together and I'd
          like to work on that. Just like
          we'd like to work on how you have
          financial issues.

                    BARRY
               (to Larry)
          She means all the lending. And the
          borrowing...

                    LARRY
          I know what she meant.

EXT. POOLSIDE - CONTINUOUS

Ronnie, Jason, and Desi talk.

                    JASON
          You are a beautiful woman, but you
          are not totally maxed out. I would
          say honestly, you're a six. Six and
          a half. I could make you an eleven.

                    DESI
          Really?

                    JASON
          When I found Deb, she was a seven.
          And now she's a twelve.

                    DESI
          I want to be a twelve.

                    JASON
          You can't be lazy.

                    DESI
          I don't want to be lazy.

                    JASON
          Look at me. You cannot be lazy.

                    DESI
          I won't be lazy.

                    JASON
Do you know how she got her body?
Bodies By Jason.

                    DESI
Wow.

                    JASON
Say it.

                    DESI
Bodies By Jason.

                    JASON
Say it again.

                    DESI
Bodies By Jason.

                    JASON
And now just say Jason.

                    DESI
Jason.

                    JASON
Again?

                    DESI
        (whispers)
Jason.

                    JASON
That sounds right, doesn't it?

                    DESI
Yeah.

                    RONNIE
What the fuck is happening right
now?

EXT. BACKYARD - CONTINUOUS

                    LARRY
When was the last time you two saw
each other, if you don't mind me
asking?

                    OLIVER
Actually, we had lunch together
last week.

                    LARRY
And before that?

                    OLIVER
It's been about seven years.

                    LARRY
Seven years? That's a joke, right?
That's like two Olympics. And I'm
the bad guy. What Debbie doesn't
understand is that it's not bad to
help out a parent. And it's
certainly not bad for a parent to
help out a child. I'm sure Oliver
would agree.

                    DEBBIE
Are you really doing this right
now?

                    LARRY
Am I doing what? I didn't start the
toast.

                    DEBBIE
Are you really about to hit up my
dad for money?

                    LARRY
What? He does four operations a
day. It's perfect. It helps
everybody, and it relieves his
guilt from all the abandonment
issues.

                    DEBBIE
You can't buy forgiveness, right
Pete?

                    PETE
I don't think anyone's looking for
handouts... We'd pay him back.

                    OLIVER
If you two are in a bind I'd be
more than happy to help.

                    DEBBIE
No. It's not good to borrow money
from family members because it
causes resentment, remember?

                    PETE
Yeah.

                    LARRY
What do you want me to do? Admit
that my life is shit? Is that what
you want me to say? You happy?
Aren't I allowed a little joy with
these children I never wanted to
have?

                    DEBBIE
You have never once stopped asking
us for money.

                    LARRY
Family helps family.

                    PETE
It's true. Family helps family.
Look, I don't expect you to fully
understand. Your dad left. You're
broken inside. It's not your fault
you can't feel love. There's
something that you can't -- this is
coming out wrong.

                    DEBBIE
You know what? I would rather have
my dad than your dad, because he
doesn't drive me crazy. You know
the best quality my father has? He
asks for nothing. I don't know what
the fuck he's thinking right now.
Look at that. Nothing. I don't even
know him. And I turned out
perfectly fine without his input.

                    LARRY
I just figured out what your
problem is. You hate Jews. Which is
so odd because your children are
Jewish.

                    DEBBIE
Don't play the Jew card, Larry.

                    LARRY
I'm not playing any Jew card.

                    DEBBIE
Seriously, it's used up.

                    LARRY
You can't use up a Jew card. That's
the whole point of a Jew card.

                    BARRY
          That's right. You can't use it up,
          it goes forever.

                    OLIVER
          You know what? I have to go.

Oliver gets up to leave.

                    PETE
          Great. What a big surprise. Bye
          Oliver. See you later. See you in
          another seven years. Make sure to
          say goodbye to the grandkids, who
          you met today. You know, nothing I
          do is right because of you?
          Nothing. No matter how hard I try,
          I'm just the asshole here, but you
          know what I realized? It's you.
          You're the asshole.

                    OLIVER
          Good luck working that out. Happy
          birthday and go fuck yourself.

Oliver walks out.

                    LARRY
          See you when the Cubs win the
          Pennant.

                    BARB
          I'm going to light the candles. Get
          it going.

                    LARRY
          Maybe we should try the toast
          again.

                    DEBBIE
          Can you be quiet?
             (to Pete)
          You just threw me under the bus.

                    PETE
          No. We agreed to let go and
          forgive, but then you started
          ripping into my dad like a crazy
          person.

                    DEBBIE
          I'm not ripping into your dad. I'm
          just saying to him what you say to
          me.

                    PETE
          Don't be such a ball buster.

                    DEBBIE
          I am not a ball buster. You make me
          one! I am a fun girl! I am fun-
          loving! I am a good time Sally! I
          dance hip-hop. I cannot believe
          I've wasted my whole life busting
          the balls of people who have no
          balls. I am the only one here who
          has any balls.

EXT. BACKYARD - DAY

Graham Parker sings "Happy Birthday" to Pete as Charlotte
accompanies him on a keyboard. The party is tense.

Debbie looks over and sees that Oliver never actually left.
He stands in the back looking uncomfortable, quietly singing.
She's shocked he's still there.

EXT. HOUSE - DAY - LATER

Debbie smokes a cigarette at the side of the house. Sadie
appears.

                    SADIE
          Mom?

Debbie turns, caught.

                    SADIE (CONT'D)
          Mom! What are you doing?

                    DEBBIE
          What?

                    SADIE
          You're smoking? In the front yard?

                    DEBBIE
          No, they're Barb's.

She walks away towards the house. Sadie follows.

INT./EXT. FOYER - CONTINUOUS

Sadie storms through the front door after Debbie.

                    SADIE
          Mom! Since when have you been a
          smoker?

                    DEBBIE
          I'm not a smoker.

Debbie keeps walking down the hall. Sadie follows her.

                    SADIE
          I thought you said smokers die.

                    DEBBIE
          I wasn't smoking.

                    SADIE
          I saw you.

Barb is in the kitchen with Pete and Charlotte.

                    CHARLOTTE
          Mom, you're smoking?

                    BARB
          Deb, you can't smoke, you're
          pregnant. You've been doing so
          well.

                    CHARLOTTE
          You're pregnant?

                    SADIE
          No f-ing way. I don't want another
          sister.

                    CHARLOTTE
          I don't want her as a sister.

                    BARB
          I'm sorry. I'm so sorry. It just
          slipped out.

Debbie turns the corner to find Pete standing in front of the
fridge, stress eating.

                    PETE
               (mouth full of cupcake)
          Are you really pregnant? Since when
          are you pregnant?

                    DEBBIE
          Since when do you care? You don't
          want another baby.

                    PETE
You have no idea what I want.

                    CHARLOTTE
I want an Asian baby.

                    SADIE
We're not going to have an Asian
baby.

                    CHARLOTTE
Yes, we are!

                    SADIE
They're not Asian.

                    DEBBIE
Sadie.

                    CHARLOTTE
We'll buy one.

                    SADIE
Shut up, Charlotte.

                    CHARLOTTE
You shut up!

                    DEBBIE
Shut up, Sadie!

                    SADIE
Shut up, Charlotte!

                    CHARLOTTE
Shut up!

                    DEBBIE
Okay, Sadie. Shut up.

                    SADIE
Shut up, Charlotte!

                    DEBBIE
Okay, stop saying shut up!

                    PETE
Since when are you pregnant? When
did you find out?

                    DEBBIE
Will you stop eating cupcakes,
please! Stop eating cupcakes. Stop
eating cupcakes!!

Debbie storms off back towards the foyer. Larry pops out from the living room, stopping Debbie in the foyer. Claire and the triplets are right behind him.

> LARRY
> Hey! We just heard. You're having a baby! See, it can happen to anybody.

> CLAIRE
> That is so wonderful. We're so happy for you.

INT. KITCHEN - CONTINUOUS

Pete throws his cupcake against the wall.

> SADIE
> (to Charlotte)
> This is too adult for you. Let's go outside.

INT. FOYER - CONTINUOUS

Larry and Claire walk away as Pete storms in.

> DEBBIE
> Well, I guess we're stuck together forever, then, right?

> PETE
> Weren't we always?

> DEBBIE
> You don't even want a baby.

> PETE
> Of course I do. I never said that. Look, I didn't want one if I could choose.

> DEBBIE
> I should put that on a Hallmark card. That's beautiful.

Oliver passes Pete and turns to Debbie as Pete walks away.

> OLIVER
> Good luck with the pregnancy, Debbie. But please, take care of yourself. It's a much riskier pregnancy after forty.

                    DEBBIE
          I'm not forty.

                    OLIVER
          Of course you are. You were born on
          December 5th, 1972.

                    DEBBIE
          How do you know?

                    OLIVER
          I was there. I'm the one who took
          your mother to the hospital.

                    DEBBIE
          That's not what she said.

                    OLIVER
          Your mom was in labor for only
          twenty minutes. It was like you
          couldn't wait to meet me, can you
          imagine that?

Debbie is stunned.

                    DEBBIE
          I don't even know you. You can't
          just come into my house and
          reminisce.

                    OLIVER
               (walking out)
          Look, maybe we were just not meant
          to be in each other's lives. I'm
          not sure this was such a great
          idea.

Debbie follows him out the door and onto the front porch. She
closes the door behind them.

EXT. FRONT PORCH - CONTINUOUS

                    DEBBIE
          Hey, wait a minute. You did leave.
          And you didn't come back.

                    OLIVER
               (getting agitated)
          My first life was ruined. I did my
          best with my second.

                    DEBBIE
          So I ruined your life? I was eight.

                    OLIVER
          People do better when I stay out of
          their lives. That's what my son
          tells me. You think my life is so
          perfect? I've got a thirteen-year-
          old who's a pot head, I've got a
          wife who's keeping Zoloft alive.

                    DEBBIE
          You never said that before.

                    OLIVER
          You don't think I want to talk to
          you about this? To share it with
          you? It's just not our way! We
          don't talk to each other, we don't
          know each other. I thought that's
          the way you wanted it. How do I get
          out of this? How do I get you all
          to just help me down off the cross?

Debbie looks at him for a moment.

                    DEBBIE
          You sound just like Sadie.

                    OLIVER
          Who's Sadie? No. Your daughter,
          your younger?

                    DEBBIE
          The big one.

                    OLIVER
          Your older. I know that! She's a
          wonderful girl.

Larry opens the door and peeks out. We reveal that everyone
at the party (except Pete) is still standing in the foyer.

                    LARRY
          Hi, guys. Some of us need to leave.
          Would this be a good moment to
          sneak out?

From the side of the house we see Pete storming by on his
bike, wearing his street clothes and a helmet.

                    SADIE
          Where's Dad going?

EXT. CITY STREETS - DAY

Pete exits his home riding his bike. He is very angry. He
rides with great emotion like he is trying to get all the
frustration out of his body.

                    PETE
          Best birthday ever!

Pete rides his bike onto San Vicente Boulevard.

Pete rides down the street. A CAR passes by him. When it does
a fifteen-year-old TEENAGER sticks his head out the window
and yells to scare Pete.

                    TEENAGER
          Bike lane, asshole!

Pete almost falls.

                    PETE
          Fuck you, you *Twilight* pimply-ass
          motherfuckers!

INT. KITCHEN - DAY

Debbie and Barb are cleaning up. They look out the window to
see Oliver picking up glasses and putting them in a bin.

                    BARB
          Your dad's still here.

                    DEBBIE
          I know. It's weird. Where the hell
          is Pete?

Sadie walks in with Joseph.

                    SADIE
          Mom, is it okay if Joseph hangs out
          here for a while?

                    DEBBIE
          Sure. Hi, Joseph.

                    JOSEPH
          Hi.

                    DEBBIE
          Do you want a piece of cake?

                    JOSEPH
          Oh, yeah sure. Thank you.

Sadie walks off.

                    JOSEPH (CONT'D)
          All right, then.

Joseph follows.

                    BARB
          They are so cute.

                    DEBBIE
          So cute.

                    BARB
          He looks exactly like Tom Petty.

EXT. STREET - DAY

There is no bike lane and cars going very fast have to swerve
to avoid Pete. A car honks when traffic clogs up behind him.

                    PETE
          Go around!

A car makes a right turn, and Pete almost rides right into
it.

                    PETE (CONT'D)
          Watch it!

He pulls up alongside Jason's van. Desi is riding with Jason.

                    DESI
          Hey, Pete. Great party!

They speed off.

                    PETE
          Yeah. The best!

EXT. BACKYARD - DAY

Oliver and the kids are playing with an iPhone.

                    SADIE
          Then you shake it. And then a
          restaurant comes up.

Debbie walks outside.

                    DEBBIE
          Dad? Excuse me. I'm going to go
          look for Pete. Would you mind
          staying with the girls for just a
          little bit?

                    OLIVER
               (shocked)
          Well, if you want me to.

                    DEBBIE
          If you don't mind. You don't have
          to.

                    OLIVER
          Sure.
               (beat)
          Can I let Sadie show me the last
          episode of *Lost*? She asked me if
          I'd seen it, I haven't.

                    DEBBIE
          That would be nice. Thank you.

                    OLIVER
          Thank you.

Debbie exits.

                    OLIVER (CONT'D)
               (to Sadie)
          She said we could watch it.

Sadie turns to Charlotte, puts her arm around her.

                    SADIE
          I'm going to let you watch *Lost*.
          Come on.

Charlotte smiles, delighted to be accepted by her sister.

                    CHARLOTTE
          Is it scary?

                    SADIE
          I'll cover your eyes if it gets too
          scary.

EXT. STREET - DAY

Pete starts riding really fast and passes a car. When the car
stops for a red he keeps going, tears off to the left,
crosses four lanes of traffic in both directions and almost
gets hit.

Pete rides his bike up a steep hill.

He passes some other bikers almost hitting them.

INT. DEBBIE'S CAR - DAY

Debbie drives around the neighborhood with Larry in the
passenger seat.

                    LARRY
          Are you mad at me? Did I say
          something?

                    DEBBIE
          Shh. Larry, please.

EXT. STREET - DAY

Pete flies down a steep hill going crazy fast. Close up of
his front wheel shaking. It is as if he wants to crash.

He rides down the street when suddenly a MAN IN A RANGE ROVER
opens his door to exit his car and Pete slams directly into
the man's car door -- hard, breaking the man's window and
falling to the ground.

The man is an incredibly thick fifty-five-year-old.

                    MAN IN RANGE ROVER
          Are you fucking kidding me?

                    PETE
          You opened your door on me.

                    MAN IN RANGE ROVER
          I didn't open my fucking door on
          you. I opened my door!

Pete slowly gets to his feet.

                    PETE
          I was right there! You are supposed
          to look before you open your door.
          I was in the fucking bike path.

>   MAN IN RANGE ROVER
> That's a blind spot. There's no
> fucking bike path. This is a
> residential section. Get your head
> out of your ass.

>   PETE
> Pay attention!

>   MAN IN RANGE ROVER
> Open your god damn eyes. What are
> you doing, sleepwalking?

>   PETE
> You're supposed to look to see if a
> biker is coming through. You're
> supposed to look!

>   MAN IN RANGE ROVER
> It's not my job to look out for
> you. You look out for yourself. I
> don't look out for you. I don't see
> you. I don't now where the fuck you
> are and what you're doing.

>   PETE
> No one is ever looking out for me!

>   MAN IN RANGE ROVER
> I need your name and number.

>   PETE
> Why?

>   MAN IN RANGE ROVER
> Because you're going to pay for my
> door.

INT. DEBBIE'S CAR - CONTINUOUS

They drive near the scene of Pete's accident and overhear.

>   PETE (O.S.)
> Fuck you!

EXT. STREET - CONTINUOUS

>   PETE
> Why don't you pay for my bike --
> and my face, you fucking prick!

The man punches Pete in the face where he's already bleeding.

INT. DEBBIE'S CAR

Debbie sees the punch and gasps, realizing it's Pete.

EXT. STREET- CONTINUOUS

Pete looks stunned.

He punches the man in the gut, to no effect. The man punches
Pete back in the stomach. Pete sinks to the ground.

                    MAN IN RANGE ROVER
              Don't disrespect me.

INT. DEBBIE'S CAR - CONTINUOUS

Debbie watches Pete fall to the ground. She opens the car
door and starts to run over toward him.

                    LARRY
              Are you sure that's him? I don't
              think that's him.

EXT. STREET- CONTINUOUS

As the man starts his engine, Debbie runs toward Pete.

                    PETE
                 (in pain)
              I'm going to write down your
              license plate number.

The car drives away, revealing that it is new and has
dealer's plates with no numbers.

                    PETE (CONT'D)
              "Range Rover of Sunland."

Debbie reaches him and holds his head up.

                    DEBBIE
              What are you doing?

                    PETE
              Ow.

INT. HOSPITAL - NIGHT

Debbie and Larry sit in the waiting area of the hospital.

                    LARRY
          I guess the party didn't turn out
          like you planned.

                    DEBBIE
          It wasn't a good party.

A NURSE walks over to them.

                    NURSE
          Hi. I'll bring you in as soon as
          his x-rays are finished.

                    DEBBIE
          Is he okay?

                    NURSE
          Yeah, he has a broken rib and he's
          been crying a little bit, but he'll
          be fine.

The Nurse walks away.

                    LARRY
          You know Pete was never a real
          fighter. But that's why he married
          you. That's why he loves you.
          Because you're the fighter, and you
          need that. One person in a
          relationship has got to punch.

                    DEBBIE
          Do you mean that in a good way?

                    LARRY
          Oh, it's a high compliment.

                    DEBBIE
          Thanks.

                    LARRY
          Listen, I know what you're worried
          about. You think he's going to turn
          into me, but I don't think it's
          going to happen. He's smarter and
          probably a little cuter. A little
          less Jewy. Although, after fifty,
          that's all going to change. Be
          prepared to wake up one day with a
          a rabbi. But the good news is,
          he'll love you forever. That's in
          our DNA. We stick around.

                    DEBBIE
          He worries about you. It puts a lot
          of pressure on him.

                    LARRY
          I know. I just don't have anyone
          else to talk to about it.

                    DEBBIE
          You can talk to Claire.

                    LARRY
          No. If I open up to her she'll
          leave me.

                    DEBBIE
          No, she won't, Larry, she loves
          you.

                    LARRY
          I know, but there's a certain point
          at which you just can't stay.
               (beat)
          I guess it's hard to forgive
          somebody if they don't formally
          apologize to you.

                    DEBBIE
          Are you apologizing?

                    LARRY
          I'm very close.
               (beat)
          Yes, I'm sorry. And I'm glad
          everybody's okay.

                    DEBBIE
          Thanks.

She hugs him and starts to cry a little bit.

                    LARRY
          I'm off.

                    DEBBIE
          Okay.

                    LARRY
          This is awkward.

                    DEBBIE
          What?

                    LARRY
          I need forty dollars for a cab.

                    DEBBIE
               (laughing)
          That's funny.

                    LARRY
          No, I'm not kidding. You drove me.
          I wasn't prepared.

                    DEBBIE
          I only have a hundred.

                    LARRY
          That's okay. I'll bring you the
          change.

He grabs the bill out of her purse and walks off.

                    LARRY (CONT'D)
          All right, give him a kiss for me.

INT. HOUSE - NIGHT

Oliver is sitting on the couch with Charlotte and Sadie
watching the last scene of *Lost*. Joseph has joined them.

                    OLIVER
          I don't get it.

                    SADIE
          See, it's not sad, it's happy
          because they helped each other
          achieve their destiny.

                    OLIVER
          Oh.

                    CHARLOTTE
          Great. I'm going to have some
          freaky ass nightmares.

INT. HOSPITAL ROOM - NIGHT

Debbie walks into Pete's room, sits on the bed next to him.

                    DEBBIE
          I really liked our lives so much
          better before we tried to change
          everything. I'm sorry.

                    PETE
No. I'm sorry. I don't want to keep
anything from you. I love you.
You're my wife. I just didn't want
to let you down.

                    DEBBIE
Are you mad that I'm pregnant?

                    PETE
No. I'm not mad. I'm thrilled.

                    DEBBIE
You don't feel trapped?

                    PETE
Sometimes I feel like I trapped
you.

                    DEBBIE
I don't feel trapped.

                    PETE
Really?

                    DEBBIE
No.

                    PETE
You should, because I've trapped
you. You can't go anywhere. I'm
going to get you pregnant every ten
years for the rest of your life.
You can never leave me. Ever.

                    DEBBIE
I never feel trapped by you. I'm so
happy to be with you. I love you so
much. You're my favorite person in
the whole world. God damn it, why
am I crying like this? Something is
wrong with me.

                    PETE
You're pregnant.

                    DEBBIE
Oh, yeah. Shit. I was just outside
telling your dad that I liked him.
What if he thinks I like him now?

                    PETE
No, he won't think that.

                    DEBBIE
I don't want him to think I like
him that much.

                    PETE
It'll never happen.

                    DEBBIE
          (suddenly giddy)
Can you believe it? This is the
craziest thing ever. What are we
going to do with a third baby?

                    PETE
I have no idea. How are we going to
afford it?

                    DEBBIE
We'll sell the house.

                    PETE
We don't have to.

                    DEBBIE
We kind of do.

                    PETE
We kind of do.

                    DEBBIE
We'll make new memories in a new
house.

                    PETE
I love you.

                    DEBBIE
Is there anything you want to do
for your birthday? It's been the
worst birthday ever.

                    PETE
There is one thing, but I don't
think you'll like it.

                    DEBBIE
What?

                    PETE
I wouldn't mind going to see some
music. Would you want to do that?

                    DEBBIE
Yeah.

                    PETE
          Really? I don't believe you, but
          you're sweet for saying that.

                    DEBBIE
          How do we break you out of here?

                    PETE
          I can just leave on my own
          volition. It's not a mental
          institution.

                    DEBBIE
          Can you?

                    PETE
          It's not like *One Flew Over the
          Cuckoo's Nest*. Please don't put a
          pillow over my face.

Debbie laughs.

                    DEBBIE
          Let's get out of here, McMurphy.

                    PETE
          You got it, Chief. Will you carry
          me?

As Debbie helps Pete off of the hospital bed, Pete kisses her
passionately.

INT. SMALL NIGHTCLUB - NIGHT

Pete and Debbie watch Ryan Adams perform "Lucky Now" with his
band.

                    DEBBIE
          I like this song.

                    PETE
          Really?

                    DEBBIE
          Yeah. Why?

Pete smiles.

                    DEBBIE (CONT'D)
          Why don't you sign him?

                    PETE
          Ryan Adams? No, he wouldn't sign
          with me.

                    DEBBIE
          Why not? You're the best.

She smiles at him and he smiles back, almost blushing. This
is the smile he has been waiting for.

                    PETE
          Well, he is in between labels.
          Let's go try and talk to him after
          the show.

The camera pulls back as Ryan Adams finishes his song.

FADE TO BLACK

AFTERWORD

MY PROCESS AS WRITER/DIRECTOR
BY JUDD APATOW

My filmmaking approach is quite simple.

I think it is very important to have a rock-solid script. Once that is achieved (after many years), we do a lot of rehearsals where we explore the emotional life of the story. I videotape these sessions. Then I take another pass, and we do a table-read with as many smart friends as I can gather so they can hear it and offer criticism. Followed by another pass. Then we do a longer rehearsal where play is encouraged. I also have the actors read all of the dialogue I cut out of drafts to see if anything is worth shooting.

Then I do another pass.

Then another table-read.

Then another pass.

When it is time to shoot the movie, I always shoot the scene until I feel like it is working both emotionally and comedically. Then I try out some alternate lines I feed to the actor. At the end of each setup I open it up for a few takes where we loosen up the dialogue and let the actors explore.

People love to ask about improv, but the truth is the main purpose of improvisation is to force actors to be in the moment. How can you be out of the moment if you are not sure exactly what your scene partner might say next? Occasionally this results in some great lines and inspired moments, but its main importance is that it improves performance.

Sometimes I get alternate material that helps me have the flexibility to move scenes to different time frames in the story if I decide in post that it is needed. I even shot a couple of scenes in two different outfits so I would have the ability to change the scene's location in the story if I had to.

The last thing I shoot is material that I call "the reshoot during the shoot." In the morning, I always take a few minutes to think, *If this scene came out terribly, what would I have done wrong?*

Then, when I finish the scene, I try to shoot some alts to fix that problem in post. If a line feels like I might find it too sentimental in editing six months in the future, I might get an alternative line that is less so. If an actor yells a lot in a scene, and I worry that it MAY be too much, I might do a take where the actor doesn't yell. I have never done reshoots on movies I have directed as a result of this technique. Or, one might say I have done the equivalent of eight days of reshoots on every movie I have ever made.

During post I like to do a lot of tests. Sometimes I test two different cuts at the same time in different theaters. Over the course of many screenings I try out all of my favorite jokes and different versions of scenes and story structures. The main purpose of the tests is to make sure the film is both funny and emotionally truthful. At this point I am trying to make sure I have followed through on my original intentions when I first thought of the idea.

We also obsessively fix dialogue by writing lines that play on the back of characters' heads. When one of these last-minute saves gets a big laugh, I feel great joy and relief. I believe Clint Eastwood saying, "Do you feel lucky punk?" was said on the back of his head. I am not sure if it was punched up in post. Possibly the original on-camera line was, "So please don't make trouble, I think this will work best if we both respect each other's feelings."

There you have it. Now you try!

CAST AND CREW CREDITS

UNIVERSAL PICTURES Presents

An APATOW Production of A JUDD APATOW Film

PAUL RUDD LESLIE MANN JOHN LITHGOW MEGAN FOX MAUDE APATOW CHRIS O'DOWD

JASON SEGEL MELISSA McCARTHY GRAHAM PARKER and ALBERT BROOKS

"THIS IS 40"

LENA DUNHAM ANNIE MUMOLO ROBERT SMIGEL CHARLYNE YI LISA DARR

Written and Directed by JUDD APATOW	Director of Photography PHEDON PAPAMICHAEL A.S.C.	Music Supervisor JONATHAN KARP
Based on Characters Created by JUDD APATOW	Production Designer JEFFERSON SAGE	Casting by ALLISON JONES
Produced by JUDD APATOW BARRY MENDEL CLAYTON TOWNSEND	Edited by BRENT WHITE A.C.E. JAY DEUBY DAVID BERTMAN	Costume Designer LEESA EVANS Co-Producer LISA YADAVAIA
Executive Producer PAULA PELL	Music by JON BRION	

CAST

(in order of appearance)

Pete . . . . PAUL RUDD
Debbie . . . . LESLIE MANN
Sadie . . . . MAUDE APATOW
Charlotte . . . . IRIS APATOW
Jason . . . . JASON SEGEL
Barb . . . . ANNIE MUMOLO
Barry . . . . ROBERT SMIGEL
Desi . . . . MEGAN FOX
Jodi . . . . CHARLYNE YI
Male Boutique Customer . . . . . HUGH FINK
Himself . . . . GRAHAM PARKER
Graham Parker Solo Band . . . TOM FREUND
Older Pregnant Parent . . . . D.A. SANDOVAL
School Playdate Parent . . . MEGAN GRANO
School Playdate Child
. . . . MACKENZIE ALADJEM
Charlotte's Teacher . . . . TOM YI
Grandma Molly . . . . MOLLY SHAD
Accountant . . . . . . MICHAEL IAN BLACK
Ronnie . . . . CHRIS O'DOWD
Cat . . . . LENA DUNHAM
Jewish Journal Reporter . . . . . . DAVID WILD
Mammogram Tech . . . BARB HERNANDEZ
Pete's Doctor . . . . TOM EVERETT
Dr. Pellegrino . . . . TIM BAGLEY
Colonoscopy Technician . DAMON GUPTON

Dentist . . . . DAN BAKKEDAHL
Gyno Nurses . . . . REBEKKA JOHNSON
ERICA VITTINA PHILLIPS
Larry . . . . ALBERT BROOKS
Triplets . . . . JACK METCALF
TRAVIS METCALF
BRADLEY METCALF
Claire . . . . LISA DARR
Oliver . . . . JOHN LITHGOW
Room Service Waiters
. . . . JOHNNY PEMBERTON
DEREK BASCO
Eastern Doctor . . . . SAM DISSANAYAKE
Realtor. . . . . TATUM O'NEAL
Wendy . . . . AVA SAMBORA
Sadie's Set-Painting Friend . . NYLA DURDIN
Joseph . . . . RYAN LEE
Flirty Hockey Player . . . . . WYATT RUSSELL
Hockey Player . . . . PHIL BURKE
Himself . . . . R. MATT CARLE
Himself . . . . IAN LAPERRIÈRE
Himself . . . . JAMES F. VANRIEMSDYK
Himself . . . . . SCOTT WESLEY HARTNELL
The Rumour Band . . . . STEVE GOULDING
ANDREW BODNAR
MARTIN BELMONT
BOB ANDREWS
BRINSLEY SCHWARZ

Himself . . . . BILLIE JOE ARMSTRONG
Catherine . . . . MELISSA MCCARTHY
Vice Principal Laviani . . . . JOANNE BARON
Obnoxious Teenagers in SUV
. . . . SPENCER DANIELS
CHARLOTTE TOWNSEND
Man in Range Rover . . . . . . PHIL HENDRIE
E.R. Nurse . . . . NICOL PAONE
Himself . . . . RYAN ADAMS
Ryan Adams Band . . . . CHRIS STILLS
IAN MCLAGAN
MARSHALL VORE
CINDY CASHDOLLAR
GUS SEYFFERT

Stunt Coordinator . . . . JOEL KRAMER
Stunts . . . . COLIN FOLLENWEIDER,
MARK AARON WAGNER, GARY
HANSON, PAUL LANE, JOE BUCARO,
JOEL MICHAEL KRAMER, NORMAN
HOWELL, DEBBIE EVANS, TOM ELLIOTT,
TIERRE RAMONE TURNER, STEVE
HART, RILEY HARPER, JACK
CARPENTER, NICK STANNER, STEVE
SCHRIVER, DICK ZIKER, WALLY
CROWDER, SCOTT LEVA, JODY MILLARD

CREW

Unit Production Managers . . . . . Charles Newirth
Production Manager
. . . . CLAYTON TOWNSEND
First Assistant Director. . MATT REBENKOFF
Second Assistant Director . . PAUL SCHNEIDER

Additional Editors. MELISSA BRETHERTON
PAUL ZUCKER

Production Supervisor
. . . . BARRETT KLAUSMAN

Art Director . . . . . . ANDREW MAX CAHN
Assistant Art Director . . . . BRADLEY RUBIN
Set Decorator . . . . LESLIE POPE
Art Department Coordinators. . . ARI JACOBS
LIBARKIN, AMANDA BROMBERG
Lead Set Designer . . . . JAMES TOCCI
Set Designer . . . . STELLA VACCARO
Graphic Designers . . . . . CHRISTA MUNRO,
ANDREW CAMPBELL
Property Master . . . . SEAN MANNION
Assistant Property Master . . MICHAEL GLYNN
Property Assistant . . . . . JEFFRY VOORHEES
Leadman . . . . RUSSELL ANDERSON

Buyer . . . . HELEN KOZORA-TELL
Set Dressers . . . . TONY ANDRAUS,
MATTHEW ATZENHOFFER, SCOTT
HUKE, DAVID LADISH, JOE
PFALTZGRAF, ERIK POLCZWARTEK
On Set Dresser . . . . . MARCUS AURALIUS
A Camera Operator/Steadicam
. . . . DAVID LUCKENBACH
B Camera Operator . . . . TARI SEGAL
1st Assistant A Camera . . . TREVOR LOOMIS
2nd Assistant A Camera . . MARK CONNELLY
2nd 2nd Assistant A Camera . . . . JAY HAGER
1st Assistant B Camera . . . . . . JEFF PORTER
2nd Assistant B Camera . . MARTIN MOODY
Underwater DP/Operator . . MIKE THOMAS
1st Assistant Underwater Camera . . PETER LEE
Aerial Director of Photography
. . . . HANS BJERNO
Digital Imaging Technician
. . . . SARAH BRANDES
Sound Mixer . . . . KEN MCLAUGHLIN
Boom Operator . . . . SCOTT JACOBS
Utility Sound . . . . CHRIS DIAMOND
Script Supervisor. . . . VALERIA M. COLLINS
Chief Lighting Technician
. . . . RAFAEL SANCHEZ
Asst. Chief Lighting Technician
. . . . SCOTT SPRAGUE
Dimmerboard Operator
. . . . JOSHUA THATCHER
Lighting Technicians . . . . . ALEX CASTILLO,
DANIEL GONZALEZ, LUKAS HENCEY,
CHRIS MILANI, LUIS MORENO,
FRANCINE NATALE, SIMONE PERUSSE,
CHRIS WEIGAND
Rigging Chief Lighting Technician
. . . . SCOTT GRAVES
Asst. Rigging Chief Lighting Tech.
. . . . GREG LOPEZ
Special Op/Fixtures . . . . . . MIKE VISENCIO
Rigging Lighting Technicians . . . . . . STEVEN
CASTANEDA, JERRY GREGORICKA,
AARON RICHARDS, JOEL RUIZ,
MICHAEL LYON
Key Grip . . . . J. MICHAEL POPOVICH
Best Boy Grip . . . . JOHN MILLER
A Dolly Grip . . . . JASON TALBERT
B Dolly Grip . . . . MICHAEL DUARTE
Grips . . . . JON JACOB FUNK,
TODD GERITZ, RICHARD JONES,
STEVEN SERNA, SATOSHI YAMAZAKI
Key Rigging Grip . . . . . JERRY SANDAGER
Best Boy Rigging Grip
. . . . ANTHONY MOLLICONE

Rigging Grips . . . . CHAD DIEKMANN, DAVID GONZALEZ, TED KENNEDY, DAMON WIERBILIS
Special Effects Coordinator . . . . DONALD FRAZEE
Special Effects Technician . . . ROBERT COLE
Costume Supervisor . . . . . JOHN BRONSON
Assistant Costume Supervisor . . . . KATHERINE HAUGH
Key Costumers . . . . LIZETTE KILMER, NICOLA CLEGG
Set Costumers JENNIFER DA COSTA WOLF
Set Costumers/Buyers . . . . CARRIE HOLLINGER, ALANA STONE KAREN ANN BAIRD, MICHAEL CROW
Head Makeup Artist . . KIMBERLY GREENE
Key Makeup . . . . ERIN WOOLDRIDGE
Makeup Artist to Ms. Mann . . VALLI O'REILLY
Makeup Artists to Mr. Brooks . . . . . GERALD QUIST, EDWARD FRENCH
Hair Department Head . . . LINDA ARNOLD
Key Hair Stylist . . . . MICHAEL MOORE
Hair Stylist to Ms. Mann RODNEY ORTEGA
Hairstylist . . . . TAMMY KUSIAN

Post Production Supervisor . . LISA RODGERS
Supervising Sound Editor . . . . GEORGE ANDERSON
Re-Recording Mixers . . . . MARC FISHMAN ADAM JENKINS
1st Assistant Editor . . . . ALEX HEPBURN
Assistant Editors . . . . JOSH SALZBERG, KRISTINE MCPHERSON
Apprentice Editors . . . . . . COLLIN PITTIER, KIMBERLY HUSTON
Post Production Assistant . . DAVID LEVINSON
Dialogue & ADR Supervisor . . . . TAMMY FEARING
Sound Effects Editor . . . . CINDY MARTY
Dialogue Editors . . . . JAMES MATHENY, LARRY KEMP
ADR Editor . . . . JOE SCHIFF
1st Assistant Sound Editor . . CHERIE TAMAI
ADR Assistant Editor . . . . ANNE COUK
Post Production Coordinator . . . . CHERYL A. TKACH
Location Manager . . . . BOYD WILSON
Key Assistant Location Manager . . . . JUN LIN
Assistant Location Managers . . . . JUSTIN HARROLD, JAMES SMALL CARLOS TAPIA GRULLON, JACOB TORRES
Production Coordinator . . . . ERIN LEE SAHLSTROM

Assistant Production Coordinator . . . . CARRIE OYER
Production Secretary . . . . . . BLAKE NABAVI
Script Coordinator . . . . RENEE SHORT
2nd 2nd Assistant Director . . . . KATHRYN FRANCIS TUCKER
Storyboard Artist . . . . RAY HARVIE
Video Assist . . . . JAY HUNTOON, ROBERT STERRY
Helicopter Pilot . . . . FRED NORTH
Production Accountant . . JENNIFER CLARK
1st Assistant Accountant . . . . CHRISTOPHER CIKETIC
2nd Assistant Accountants . . . . . . ALBERTINA KELLEY, DIANA MEJIA
2nd 2nd Assistant Accountant . . . . LINDSEY HENNIG
Payroll Accountant . . . . . . JULIE BERNARDS
Accounting Clerk . . . SEAN DAVID BECKER
Post Production Accountant . . . . MISSY EUSTERMANN
Casting Associate . . . . BEN HARRIS
Casting Assistant . . PETER JOHN KOUSAKIS
Extras Casting . . . . WENDY TREESE, RASHE' JOHNSON
Assistant to Mr. Apatow . . . . ALYSON BUONCRISTIANI
Assistant to Mr. Mendel . . NATE SHERMAN
Assistant to Mr. Townsend . . . . JESSICA DERHAMMER
Office Production Assistants . . . . KELLY BERTHOLD, MOLLY FERGUSON CHRISTOPHER PLUCHAR, CHARLOTTE TOWNSEND
Set Production Assistants . . . . JOANN CONNOLLY, ANGEL COOK, DAVID JENNIS, YARDEN LEVO, FRANNY STAFFORD, SHAUN WEISS, RYAN BRUNNER, ANTHONY STEINHART
Production Assistants . . . . . . K.C. SCHRIMPL, JACOB DEPP, CODY CAIRA, BRIAN BACHMAN, TAYLOR KANNETT
Art Department Assistant . . . . . ERIN RIEGEL
Construction Coordinator . . . . DAVE DEGAETANO
General Foreman . . . . . . STEVEN RIGAMAT
Drape Master . . . . BRAD CURRY
Location Foreman . . JAVIER CARRILLO JR.
Labor Foreman . . . . JOHN HILL
Paint Foreman . . . . MEG SNOW
Head Painter . . . . JOHN SNOW
Plaster Foreman . . . . DAVID FALCONER JR.
Stand-by Painter . . . BILL KAUHANE HOYT
Greens Foreman . . . . LEE RUNNELS

Transportation Coordinator. . DENNY CAIRA
Transportation Captain . . . . . . WALLY FRICK
Transportation Co-Captain . . MIKE PAINTER
D.O.T. Administration. . KAREN BATHALTER
Unit Publicist. . . . . TAMMY SANDLER
Stills Photographer
. . . . SUZANNE HANOVER, SMPSP
DVD Producer . . . . GREG COHEN
Videographer. . . . . JASON COX
Asset Coordinator . . . . LEE PEGLOW
Studio Teacher . . . . . . LOIS YAROSHEFSKY
Bike Consultant . . . . . WILLIAM FORTIER
Choreographer . . . . DANNY TEESON
Dental Consultant. . . . . ANDY LEWIS, DDS
Medical Technician . SUSIE SCHELLING, RN
Medics . . . . . ERICKA BRYCE PONIEWAZ,
ROBERT HEPBURN
SHERRI O'HARA, LVN
Animals Provided by
. . . . . BIRDS AND ANIMALS UNLIMITED
Craft Service . . . . CHANCE TASSONE,
JOSEPH MILITO, NICK PISTILLI
Caterer. . . . . FOUR STARS CATERING

ADR Voice Casting . WENDY HOFFMANN,
RANJANI BROW
ADR Mixer. . . . . GREG STEELE
ADR Recordist . . . . . GREG ZIMMERMAN
Foley Artists . . . . ANDY MALCOLM,
GORO KOYAMA
Foley Recording Mixers . . . . . DON WHITE,
JACK HEEREN
Foley Recordists . . . . . JENNA DALLA RIVA,
STEPHEN MUIR
Dubbing Recordists . . . . . . ZACK HOWARD,
TIM HOAGLAND
Music Editor. . . . . JONATHAN KARP
Featured Musicians . . . . CHRIS THILE,
NOAM PIKELNY, GABE WITCHER,
CHRIS ELDRIDGE, PAUL KOWERT,
MATT CHAMBERLIN, SUZIE KATAYAMA
Score Engineers. . . . . GREG KOLLER,
ERIC CADIEUX
Score Mixed by . . . . GREG KOLLER
Music Contractor . . . . GINA ZIMMITTI
MUSIC CONTRACTING
Score Recorded at . . . . . CAPITOL STUDIOS
Prod. Sound Remote Truck Engineers
. . . . SCOTT PEETS, TRINI ALVEREZ
Prod. Sound Monitor Engineers . . MARK REA,
RON ANONSEN
Production Playback Engineer
. . . . MARK AGOSTINO
Main Titles Designed by . . . . PICTURE MILL

Digital Intermediate . . . . COMPANY 3
Digital Film Colorist . . STEFAN SONNENFELD
Digital Intermediate Producer
. . . . ANNIE JOHNSON
Digital Conformist . . . . RUDY LOPEZ
Dolby Sound Consultant. . . . . . THOM EHLE
Camera Cranes / Dollies / Systems by
. . . . CHAPMAN / LEONARD
STUDIO EQUIPMENT, INC.

2ND UNIT
2nd Unit Director. . . . . JOEL KRAMER
Director of Photography . . JOHN LEONETTI
1st Assistant Director . . . . . SUSAN ELMORE
2nd Assistant Director . . . . PAULA JANOS

Visual Effects by . . . . LEVEL 256
Visual Effects Supervisor . SCOTT M. DAVIDS
Visual Effects Producer . . SETH KLEINBERG
VFX Coordinator . . . . . DENNIS MURILLO
CG Supervisor . . . . GIANCARLO LARI
Matte Painter. . . . . MARTIN KANSHIGE
Compositors. . . . . MICHAEL BOGEN,
MYONG CHOI, JOSHUA BOLIN, CHRIS
CHAPPELL ADAM LIMA

Visual Effects by
. . . . RHYTHM & HUES STUDIOS
Visual Effects Supervisor . . . EDWIN RIVERA
Visual Effects Producer. . KAREY MALTZAHN
Digital Supervisor . . WILLIAM TELFORD JR.
Pipeline TD . . . . ERIC BONILLA
Match Movers . . . . CHOON MING LAU,
SIEW CHEE NG, MIMI THIAN
BG Prep Artists . . . . . . MICHAEL FREVERT,
MARVIN JONES
Lighter . . . . SHAUN COMLY
Flame Artist . . . . YUKIKO ISHIWATA

SOUNDTRACK ALBUM ON
CAPITOL RECORDS

"I'M YOUR ANGEL"
Written by Yoko Ono
Performed by Yoko Ono
Courtesy of Lenono Music | Capitol Records LLC
Under license from EMI Film & Television Music

"HAPPY BIRTHDAY TO YOU"
Written by Mildred J. Hill, Patty Smith Hill
Performed by Paul Rudd, Maude Apatow
& Iris Apatow

"THE PACKAGE" from 'LOST'
Written by Michael Giacchino
Performed by Michael Giacchino
Courtesy of ABC Studios

"HEART AND SOUL"
Written by Hoagy Carmichael, Frank Loesser
Performed by Iris Apatow

"THE OFFICE THEME"
Written by Jay Ferguson
Performed by Iris Apatow

"SO SLEEPY (THE BELLS)"
Written by Fiona Apple Maggart, Alanis
Gordillo, Jason Lee, Alex Morones
Performed by Fiona Apple, featuring Jon Brion
and Punch Brothers
Produced by Jon Brion
Courtesy of Clean Slate / Epic Records
By arrangement with Sony Music Licensing

"MAGNET AND STEEL"
Written by Walter Lindsay Egan
Performed by Walter Egan
Courtesy of Columbia Records
By arrangement with Sony Music Licensing

"DEBASER"
Written by Charles Thompson
Performed by Pixies
Courtesy of 4AD

"TAKE ON ME"
Written by Magne Furuholmen, Morten
Harket, Pal Waaktaar
Performed by a-ha
Courtesy of Warner Bros. Records Inc.
By arrangement with Warner Music Group
Film & TV Licensing

"PRICE TAG"
Written by Bobby Simmons, Claude Kelly,
Lukasz Gottwald, Jessica Cornish
Performed by Jessie J
Courtesy of Universal Records
Under license from Universal Music Enterprises

"LOCAL GIRLS"
Written by Graham Parker
Performed by Graham Parker & Tom Freund

"ROMAN'S REVENGE"
Written by John Davis, Kasseem Dean, Bryan
Higgins, James Jackson, Ali Muhammad, Onika

Maraj, Marshall Mathers,
Trevor Smith, Malik Taylor
Performed by Nicki Minaj featuring Eminem
Courtesy of Cash Money Records / Universal
Records
Under license from Universal Music Enterprises
Eminem appears courtesy of Interscope Records

"ROOSTER"
Written by Jerry Cantrell
Performed by Alice In Chains
Courtesy of Columbia Records
By arrangement with Sony Music Licensing

"ALWAYS JUDGING (INSTRUMENTAL)"
Written and Performed by Norah Jones
Produced by Jon Brion
Courtesy of Blue Note Records
Under license from EMI Film & Television Music

"THUNDER AND RAIN"
Written by Graham Parker
Performed by Graham Parker & the Rumour
Courtesy of WTTW Digital Archives

"I WILL DARE"
Written by Paul Westerberg
Performed by The Replacements
Courtesy of Warner Bros. Records Inc.
By arrangement with Warner Music Group
Film & TV Licensing

"REWRITE"
Written by Paul Simon
Performed by Paul Simon
Courtesy of Hear Music
By arrangement with Concord Music Group,
Inc.

"iPHOTO HELL"
Written and Performed by Norah Jones
Courtesy of Blue Note Records
Under license from EMI Film & Television Music

"SHINING THROUGH THE DARK"
Written and Performed by Ryan Adams
Courtesy of Capitol Records / Sony Music /
PaxAmericana Recording Co.

"LUNCH BOX / ODD SOX"
Written by Paul McCartney, Linda McCartney
Performed by Wings
Courtesy of MPL Communications, Inc.

"DOCTOR"
Written by Inara George, Gregory Kurstin
Performed by The Bird And The Bee

"YOU CAN'T STOP THE BEAT" (from the
musical 'HAIRSPRAY')
Written by Marc Shaiman, Scott Wittman
Performed by Nikki Blonsky, Zac Efron,
Amanda Bynes, Elijah Kelley, John Travolta,
Queen Latifah
Courtesy of WaterTower Music

"LITTLE GUITARS"
Written by Edward Van Halen, Alex Van Halen,
Michael Anthony, David Lee Roth
Performed by Van Halen
Courtesy of Warner Bros. Records Inc.
By arrangement with Warner Music Group
Film & TV Licensing

"SO WHAT"
Written by Maude Apatow
Performed by Savannah Outen
Produced by Lyle Workman

"WE RUN THIS"
Written by Missy Elliott, Jeremiah Patrick
Lordan
Performed by Missy Elliott
Courtesy of Atlantic Recording Corp. and
Rhino Entertainment Company
By arrangement with Warner Music Group
Film & TV Licensing
Contains a sample of "APACHE" performed by
Sugarhill Gang courtesy of JR Foursome Music
/ Sanctuary Records Group Ltd.
Under license from Universal Music Enterprises

"(DANCE AND SHOUT) SHAKE YOUR
BODY DOWN TO THE GROUND"
Written by Michael Jackson, Randy Jackson
Performed by The Jacksons
Courtesy of Epic Records
By arrangement with Sony Music Licensing

"PROTECTION"
Written by Graham Parker
Performed by Graham Parker & the Rumour

"WHERE THEM GIRLS AT"
Written by Jared Cotter, Tramar Dillard, Onika
Maraj, Sandy Wilhelm, David Guetta, Juan
Salinas, Oscar Salinas, GiorgioTuinfort, Michael
Caren

Performed by David Guetta featuring Nicki
Minaj
Courtesy of What A Music Ltd / EMI Music
France
Under license from EMI Film & Television
Music
Nicki Minaj appears courtesy of Young Money
Entertainment / Cash Money Records /
Universal Motown Records

"STARS"
Written by Mercedes Seecoomar, Darren
Cumberbatch, Uzoechi Osisiomi Emenike,
Wilfred Samson Dedewo
Performed by Mercedes
Courtesy of Modest! Management and
Manajamma

"WATCH THE MOON COME DOWN"
Written by Graham Parker
Performed by Graham Parker & the Rumour
Courtesy of Mercury Records Limited
Under license from Universal Music Enterprises

"CALIFORNIA BABY"
Written by Jerry Burnham, Wayne Cook
Courtesy of APM Music

"VERGNÜGUNGSPARK"
Written by Gerhard Trede
Courtesy of APM Music

"DAYS THAT WE DIE"
Written by Loudon Wainwright III
Performed by Loudon Wainwright III
Courtesy of Snowden Music

"PARADISE BY THE DASHBOARD
LIGHT"
Written by Jim Steinman
Performed by Meat Loaf
Courtesy of Epic Records and Cleveland
International Records
By arrangement with Sony Music Licensing

"OLD DAYS"
Written by James Pankow
Performed by Chicago
Courtesy of Chicago Records II
By arrangement with Primary Wave Music

"FANTINE'S DEATH (COME TO ME)"
Written by Alain Albert Boublil, Claude Michel
Schonberg, Jean Marc Natel, Herbert Kretzmer

Performed by Original Broadway Cast "Les
Misérables"
Courtesy of Universal Classics Group
Under license from Universal Music Enterprises

"SS LOST-TANIC" from 'LOST'
Written by Michael Giacchino
Performed by Michael Giacchino
Courtesy of ABC Studios

"SICK OF YOU"
Written and Performed by Lindsey Buckingham
Produced by Jon Brion

"LIVE AND DIE"
Written and Performed by The Avett Brothers
Courtesy of American Recordings

"WHAT DO YOU LIKE?"
Written by Graham Parker
Performed by Graham Parker & Punch Brothers
Produced by Jon Brion
Punch Brothers appear courtesy of Nonesuch
Records

"VASOLINE"
Written by Dean DeLeo, Robert DeLeo, Eric
Kretz, Scott Weiland
Performed by Stone Temple Pilots
Courtesy of Atlantic Recording Corp.
By arrangement with Warner Music Group
Film & TV Licensing

"SANTERIA"
Written by Floyd Gaugh, Bradley Nowell, Eric
Wilson
Performed by Sublime
Courtesy of Geffen Records
Under license from Universal Music Enterprises

"THE WEIGHT"
Written by Robbie Robertson
Performed by The Band
Courtesy of Capitol Records, LLC
Under license from EMI Film & Television
Music

"HAPPY BIRTHDAY TO YOU"
Written by Mildred J. Hill, Patty Smith Hill
Performed by Graham Parker and Maude
Apatow

"MOAN ALL NIGHT"
Written by Noah Lit, Josh Lit, Gabriel Lit,

Emily St. Amand- Poliakoff, Wen Chang,
Stephen Clothier, Michael Garza
Performed by Noah and the MegaFauna

"DULL TOOL"
Written by Fiona Apple Maggart
Performed by Fiona Apple
Courtesy of Clean Slate / Epic Records
By arrangement with Sony Music Licensing

"MOVIN' ON" from 'LOST'
Written by Michael Giacchino
Performed by Michael Giacchino
Courtesy of ABC Studios

"LUCKY NOW"
Written and Performed by Ryan Adams
Courtesy of Capitol Records / Sony Music /
PaxAmericana Recording Co.

"I GOT YOU (At the End of the Century)"
Written by Jeff Tweedy
Performed by Wilco
Courtesy of dBpm Records

PRESENTED IN ASSOCIATION WITH
DENTSU INC.
(Obligatory end title credit)

"Lost" clip courtesy of ABC Studios.
"Graham Parker and the Rumour" clip courtesy
of WTTW Digital Archives / Historic Films
Archive, LLC.
Footage From 'Sunrise' Courtesy of Twentieth
Century Fox. All rights reserved.
Elliott Erwitt photography courtesy of Magnum
Photos.
Photographs © Garry Winogrand, courtesy
Fraenkel Gallery, San Francisco.
"Lost" poster © American Broadcast
Companies, Inc.
"Untitled 2009" painting courtesy of William J.
O'Brien.
Weegee (Arthur Fellig) images © Weegee /
International Center of Photography.
Ed Templeton art images courtesy of Ed
Templeton and Roberts & Tilton.
"The Dog Listener" by Jan Fennell © 2000 and
"Healing Your Aloneness: Finding Love and
Wholeness Through Your Inner Child" by
Erika J. Chopich and Margaret Paul © 1990
Harper Collins Publishing, Inc.
"South Park" books courtesy of Comedy
Central © 2009 & 2010. All rights reserved.

ABOUT THE AUTHORS

Judd Apatow

Initially aspiring to become a professional comedian, Judd Apatow eventually stopped performing in favor of writing. After writing on a few award shows, cable specials, *The Larry Sanders Show*, and *The Ben Stiller Show* (which he cocreated), Apatow served as an executive producer on NBC's critically acclaimed *Freaks and Geeks*. He then made his feature-film debut as a director with 2005's *The 40-Year-Old Virgin*. Cowritten by Apatow and the film's star, Steve Carell, *The 40-Year-Old Virgin* opened at No. 1 at the box office. In 2007, he directed, wrote, and produced *Knocked Up*, which grossed more than $200 million internationally. He followed this up by producing the hit comedies *Superbad, Forgetting Sarah Marshall*, and *Pineapple Express*, and writing and directing 2009's *Funny People*. Additional producing credits include *The Cable Guy, Anchorman: The Legend of Ron Burgundy*, and *Get Him to the Greek*. In 2011, he produced the most successful R-rated female comedy of all time, *Bridesmaids,* which received Oscar® nominations for Best Original Screenplay and Best Supporting Actress (Melissa McCarthy), as well as numerous other awards. Apatow is currently in production on the HBO series *Girls*, and recently produced *The Five-Year Engagement,* the latest comedy from director Nicholas Stoller.

Lena Dunham

Lena Dunham was raised in New York City by two artists. She graduated from Oberlin College with a creative writing degree in 2008. Her breakthrough 2010 feature *Tiny Furniture* won Best Narrative Feature at the 2010 South by Southwest Film Festival and an Independent Spirit Award for Best First Screenplay. In 2012, Lena starred in the Judd Apatow-produced HBO series *Girls*, which she also created, wrote for, and executive produced. The show follows the lives of four twenty-something women in Manhattan and received four 2012 Emmy® nominations, including nominations for her acting, writing, and directing. She is currently in production on the second season in New York City.